# Beyond Apollo

# Beyond Apollo

*by Barry N. Malzberg*

Faber and Faber
London

*First Published in the USA 1972*
*Published 1974*
*by Faber and Faber Limited*
*3 Queen Square London WC1*
*Printed in Great Britain by*
*Whitstable Litho, Whitstable, Kent*
*All rights reserved*

*ISBN 0 571 10510 6*

*For Joyce, Stephanie Jill and*
*Erika Cornell*
*And in memory of Herbert Finney*
*1898–8/27/61*

# RECOVERY

It is there, always—dead
Back of the bed, loosening
The fingers of your mind.

In sleep it takes you by the hair
A mile
Down until you watch, bailed out,
Your breath flattening
Into parachutes of mercury.
Speak, it says and watch,
Fluttering the air fall
Upward to the air.

It is in the mirror
When you wake
Anticipating.

It is there
Before you wake
Dancing; its hair
A wheel of hair, its hair
Afire.
You wake, the shadows just
Coming out from behind the chairs.

You try to pull that dance together
From the air.
Quit, capsized
In mere day.

*Trim Bissell: 1968*

# Beyond Apollo

# 1

I loved the Captain in my own way, although I knew that he was insane, the poor bastard. This was only partly his fault: one must consider the conditions. The conditions were intolerable. This will never work out.

# 2

In the novel I plan to write of the voyage, the Captain will be a tall, grim man with piercing eyes who has no fear of space. "Onward!" I hear him shout. "Fuck the bastards. Fuck control base; they're only a bunch of pimps for the politicians anyway. We'll make the green planet yet or plunge into the sun. Venus forever! To Venus! Shut off all the receivers now. Take no messages. Listen to nothing they have to say; they only want to lie about us to keep the administrators content. Venus or death! Death or Venus! No fear, no fear!"

He has also had, in the book, a vigorous and satisfying sex life, which lends power and credence to his curses and his very tight analysis of the personalities at control. "We will find our humanity under the gases of Venus," the Captain will say, and then the sounds of the voyage overwhelm us and momentarily he says nothing more. I sit with hands clasped, awaiting further word.

The novel, when I write it, should find a large commercial outlet. People still love to read stories of space, and here for the first time they will learn the sensational truth. Even though it is necessary for me to idealize the Captain in order to make the scheme more palatable, the novel will have great technical skill and will make use of my many vivid experiences in and out of the program. They cannot do this kind of thing to us and leave us nothing. I believe that passionately. The novel will be perhaps sixty-five thousand words long, and I will send it only to the very best publishers.

# 3

On one of these nights I dream that the Captain is falling again. He is falling through the capsule into the center of the sun. "Out," he says, "enough of this. I'm calling a halt to the bullshit before they turn me into a machine." Backed into a bulkhead, I beg him to be controlled and assume command of the voyage again, but he says he cannot because of the forces of gravity. Gravity is making him fall into the sun.

"I can't do all this myself," I cry as he begins to slither away again. "I'm only equipped to be the copilot. My certification is limited."

"I'm sorry," he says with infinite regret, disappeared to the neck now, his fine eyebrows poised as if for sex or intricate testimony. "I misjudged the whole thing totally. It is a mystery. You will have to do the best you can, Evans: find some answers of your own," and then he disappears, not saying goodbye.

The ship convulses slightly as if the Captain were excrement just cleansed.

I wonder why I do not follow my commander into the sun and be done with it, but there is no time for reflection; I have many things to do to keep the ship on course lest it miss Venus and follow the Captain into the solar region. I resolve to follow it through; perhaps this is another simulation testing my psychological strength.

# 4

The personnel in this large and rather homey institution warn me that I cannot go on this way indefinitely, that I must start acting in a reasonable fashion. "This is a convenient escape for you," they remind me, "and we've allowed it to go on as long as this because we thought you needed some compensatory adjustment, but now it must come to an end. You must grow up, Evans, face reality again. It is time. It is necessary. You must remember what happened to you. You must tell us all of this; we need the information to save others. You would not want to cause the death of a hundred others on the crews because you were too selfish to speak, would you?"

"You wouldn't send them out until I had spoken, would you?" I reply, my only response in weeks, and then I begin to laugh. I laugh heartily in a most unseemly manner and eventually the institutional personnel go away, although they are scheduled to return to me tomorrow and press me further. The routine is really quite organized. Some of them are young, but on the other hand, some of them are old. Some of them are male, but then again a good many of them are female and these, even unto the ugliest and most professionalized, I eye with vague lust, thinking about connection. I wonder if they will trade a fuck for some information but decide that their procedures are none of my affair; in addition to that, my lust is idle, idle—the magic rays from space rendered me impotent at last, which is a blessing. The fury will overtake me no more. I return to thoughts of the novel I will write, which will be my single attempt to give the full and final truth of the voyage in such a way that all those who understand will surely admire my strength.

# 5

Several thousand men applied for the project and only a few hundred were accepted. Of these hundreds, only twenty survived screening for the Venus flight and only the Captain and I were finally selected: two out of a pool of some thousand, the highest tenth of one percentile. According to the selection processes, I am the second most qualified man in the country to set foot on Venus for the first time, or at least I was at the time that the Committee made this final determination. Even retrospectively this fills me with a small glow of accomplishment—it is no small thing to have been so highly qualified—even though, at least in the case of the Captain, such a serious mistake was evidently made.

# 6

I dream I see the Captain fucking his wife. He rears over her, intolerably strong, enormously agile, plunging himself into her wastes. I have never met his wife but picture her well. "Fuck me, you bitch," he whispers, "fuck me good; tomorrow we're going into isolation for the flight and it may be *months* until I get laid again, depending upon how things work out." She smiles at him, winsome in the darkness, and squeezes her thighs reflexively. The Captain groans and discharges, falls across her in small stages like planks of wood settling, and begins to gasp. "Too fast, too fast, you bitch," he says and bites her shoulder; but there is the intimation of a smile on his face (I can move very close to them in the dark), and I see that although he is humiliated, he is also proud that he is able to come so fast. It is the mark of a real spaceman. "Bitch, bitch," the Captain murmurs, and thinking of Venus, he falls asleep against her.

# 7

In this solar system Venus is the second planet from the sun. It was discovered and labeled a planet by the most ancient astronomers, who in consultation with senior astrologers deemed it the planet of love. Men were tantalized by Venus for centuries, although the first manned expedition there did not occur until 1981.

During the middle third of the twentieth century probes conducted by remote capsules revealed nothing other than that the terrain was mysteriously concealed by thick layers of gases destructive to all biological life as we have conceived of it. This was a great disappointment to scientists who had thought that the life-system of Venus was the most likely of the other eight planets to sustain intelligent life and might even serve as an escape hatch in the event that our own planet should become overcrowded or ruined by atomic devices. It was in the hope of further information about this planet that the initial manned expedition to Venus embarked. The two men on the ship were the survivors of a rigorous selection process and testing program which had established beyond doubt that they were in the highest percentile of fitness and could be trusted to perform well on this unique and extremely well-publicized mission.

Success was particularly important in light of the unsatisfactory Mars adventure of 1976 which so shocked the administrators that explorations of the red planet were abandoned for the duration.

# 8

Nevertheless, I cannot help feeling that the disaster could have been averted. It was my fault; mere presence of mind would have controlled the situation.

"Nonsense," I should have said to the Captain. "These suicidal impulses are the result of an anxiety attack, a simple psychoneurotic reaction which can be easily controlled. Get hold of yourself. Be calm. Take the long view. In the anterior bulkhead is a cabinet containing multiple grains of disulfiamazole. Read the instructions carefully and then take a double dosage."

"We have no business out here," the Captain says anyway. "None whatsoever. I see it clearly now, more clearly than I have ever seen anything in my life. Nothing can justify this horror. I have had this insight. I have had this enormous insight into everything. Things are not worth the price we pay. They lied to us all the way through. Unless we take action, they will lie to us forever."

"Still," I say calmly, "stop raving. Be mature. Consider your responsibilities. This is no time for metaphysical and political rhetoric. Not with the course degrees for Venus to be charted so soon and another television broadcast scheduled some hours from now, in which we will show them some of the effects of lighting upon the anterior of the ship. And reminisce a bit together to give them the personal touch."

"There is nothing to be charted. We are navigated by remote control. They have given us an illusion of function to keep us from going mad."

"Still, the broadcast."

"I do not want to perform for them. I have no homilies; I do not want to be a television personality. Instead, I want to spit in their cameras and expose myself."

"There is no time for that," I say kindly. "I understand your position and am highly sympathetic, but you are the commander of this voyage and have responsibilities. Meet them; be a man."

Slowly but firmly, I exert tremendous pressure on the trembling elbow of the Captain, lead him to the cabinet, fling it open and, removing a bottle, force five grains of disulfiamazole into his distorted mouth. He receives them like cookies.

The Captain chokes, then chews thoughtfully, his features changing and shifting to their more customary content. He sighs, groans, scratches himself, a coarse amiability moving from him in slow, uneven waves.

"Thank you, Evans," the Captain says. "I feel much better, thanks to you."

"I'm glad. It was my pleasure. Anything I can do to help, I will."

"It must have been a fit, just a passing episode. A hint of strangeness overtaking me when I thought of the enormous responsibilities we carry. To land on Venus! To explore! To find another home for mankind! I feel much better now. I will plot courses. I will make deductions. I will smile when the broadcast begins and tell anecdotes of the old days in the academy."

Mumbling, he moves from the cabinet and begins swiftly to

9

work, seated in a cramped position, absorbed in logarithms or whatever other figures the computer disgorges. I sigh; Evans sighs. Evans relaxes and lets the tension drain from him, thinking how terrible it might have been if he had not assumed command of the situation; how the Captain's depression might have increased and he, throwing himself into the sun, would have brought the expedition to an abrupt halt.

# 9

I have a wife. Evans has a wife. Evans and I are the same person, but it is easier sometimes to slip into a more objective tense; there is now so little of myself I can bear that perhaps distancing is the answer. Another name for this, the institutional personnel hint, is disassociation reaction. I have a disassociation reaction. Evans has a disassociation reaction. Each of us has a disassociation reaction, but mine is stronger than his.

Evans has a wife. She is twenty-seven years old, with brown hair and eyes, and he admits that months ago he lived with and committed sexual acts upon her. He has some recollection of breasts with nipples like deadly painted eyes, a cunt which was slow to moisten but eventually enveloped him like knives. She comes to him now, a vaguely pretty girl with breasts now discreetly hidden, and touches his hand. His trembling hand, so dense against the sheets. Pity Evans. I do. He did not choose this way.

"Please," she says and then shakes her head at the ceiling as if looking for cameras. "Please tell them what you know, Harry. They have sent me to you as the last chance before they take further action. They are talking about shock, although I am not supposed to tell you that. They say that there will be special treatments and painful re-enactment therapy."

"Ah," I say. "Aha."

"They'll only force the truth from you anyway. You might as well tell them. They always get what they want anyway."

"Not quite."

"What happened, Harry? What went on? Don't tell them, then, if you don't want them to know. Let it be a secret then. But tell *me*. I can't stand this any more."

Her chin juts, reminding me of that other wedge of bone which rushed me in the night. A pitiful ploy. I think of her superficiality, how she must have been driven to this. The institutional personnel must have had at her in their own way. Perhaps someone is fucking her, opening up reservoirs of stupidity. "Please," she is saying. "Please."

"I don't think I know you," Evans says, looking past her. "You seem to feel there is a connection here, but you misunderstand. I see no relationship; it must all be in your mind. I do not understand. Evans does not understand. Neither of us understands."

He touches her anyway—the remote softness of her bare upper arm like metal beneath the surface, the bulbous thrust of her shoulder blade—and he fondles her then as if she were a bulkhead. A bulkhead with many devices. "I appreciate your interest in my situation, but there really isn't anything further to discuss at this time," Evans says and tries to push her from the communal room. "Maybe later," he says, courteous, straining to move her. She folds in layers against him, offering no real resistance, and stumbles backward toward the door. Evans halfway closes that door on her, stops when he sees that institutional staff are eyeing him solemnly like hounds, holding pencils and pieces of paper. Apparently they have been waiting outside the door all this time, awaiting the result of Evans' discussion with his wife.

"I don't think you understand any of this, ladies and gents," Evans says. "You're being conventional, mechanical. You are

**11**

treating me like an ordinary lunatic. But I have been to Venus and back; I am beyond normal motivations or procedures," and then he realizes that during the process of speaking he has in his excitement shut the door and no one has heard.

He considers opening the door again to repeat his statement but decides against it, inasmuch as he has already made this point several times in conference and on tape and does not want to be accused of forcing the issue. The door remains closed. His wife remains outside. His wife was always outside.

Evans returns to his various tasks in confinement: he must continue his notes toward the novel he will write, and there are also crossword puzzles, cryptograms, codes, anagrams, word games, bridge problems, and chess hairgrayers for him to solve. Lovely small neurasthenic tentacles for Evans, who is already gripped by so many. Putting the novel from his mind for the time being, Evans decides to find all the possible anagrams of VENUS containing four letters or more, plurals not allowed.

NEVU

VUSEN

SENVU

SUVEN

UNVES

VESUN

SNEVU

NEVU, VUSEN, SENVU, SUVEN, UNVES, VESUN, SNEVU

From far remove the Captain materializes—as he is occasionally apt to—and looks over Evans' shoulder, quizzicality and competence in his far-sighted gaze.

"You forgot Nevus," he says.

# 10

Evans conceives of himself as being in a compression chamber. Enormous gravitational forces occur on acceleration and re-entry, and his copilot's body must be prepared for massive strain. The program will assist him. Curled into a ball, his detumescent prick merrily fucking the folds of his underwear, Evans feels the pressure surround him like a towel pulled tight, feels the matrixes of his body descend toward one another yet again. This is his fourth time in the chamber; he will be in eight times altogether, each at greater pressure.

*Uff*, Evans says, feeling his consciousness depart from him like a lover, *woom*, and faints, eight gravities tearing at him like a bride. When he awakens, the training staff is grouped around him, their eyes alight with interest. "Where is the Captain?" Evans says. "Are you doing this to him as well?"

"Never mind the Captain," an elderly man says and touches Evans approvingly on the shoulder. "You go through the same things, although not at the same time. You went to eight gravities; that's very good."

"You son of a bitch," Evans says, "I'm going to turn in a report. You can't torture us for spite."

"It's the program, the preparation," the elderly man says soothingly, "now quiet"; and Evans, considerably shrunken, staggers to his feet and waddles from the chamber, his hilarious posterior jutting for all the world to see, the little knifelike slant of his abused genitals now useless within his clothing. He reminds himself that the Captain is surely surviving the training and therefore he can as well. It is all for Venus and of the highest importance.

# 11

I write a letter to the institutional staff in which I admit to everything. I confess that I did indeed murder the Captain; during a dismal sleep period when I could not stand the humming of the transistors I caught him unawares and shoved him through a disposal hatch. "I guess that the selection process did have defects. Perhaps I was not as highly qualified as you hoped me to be," I concede grudgingly.

Furthermore, I tell the staff that I am a felon, a lunatic, a criminal, a deviant. "Obviously I have totally buckled under the responsibility and imagined dangers of the Venus mission," I point out. "There is certainly very little to be said in my defense other than that I never deliberately hurt him. He was merely an object in the alley of madness. I am inferior, gentlemen, terribly inferior, but what does this make of those who selected me? Can you tolerate this margin of error in your own spirit?"

I fold the confession in quarters and shovel it under the door in little stages, like sex, waiting for the guards to read it and remove my privileges. Place me into deeper custody without even the comfort of cryptograms. Nothing seems to happen for a long time, however, and I become bored with simply waiting; I am tired enough.

I sleep. In this particular sleep I have a dream that the Captain enters fully restored and bestows a kindly hand on my shoulder. "It's not necessary for you to shield me any more, Evans," he says with enormous benignity. The Captain Transformed, Transmutated, Ascendant, he says, "I feel perfectly well now after my little journey to the sun and am ready to tell them the truth. The beneficial heat has removed that touch of arthritis in my joints which I concealed from the Committee; now I am ready to tell them everything." At that moment, leaning forward precariously toward him, knowing that at last I will get to the center of the matter and be finished, I hear the Captain say, "Oh, shit! I forgot that the sun gives you skin cancer; well, I won't have to worry about that for ten years, which is plenty of time to tell you the truth, which is—" and I wake from the dream to find that the lights in my quarters are still fresh and that the confession meant for the institutional staff remains. It clings perilously by an uplifted corner to the underside of the door. No one has taken it. There were no guards after all, or at least no night patrol. Perhaps they have decided that I am harmless. In any event, no one is interested.

I retrieve the confession, therefore. Now I revise it completely and in line with the ultimate, undeniable truth: I tell them that the Captain poisoned the food supplies and thus made our hands unsteady, driving the ship off course and finally killing himself for fear of apprehension; but the fact is that I do not like this any better than the other approach and so in due course toward the dawn I destroy both copies.

Shredded, in the disposal unit and ready for evacuation, the papers whirl in the flush like the spokes of constellations.

# 12

I see the Captain in the compression chamber. His features do not change. The gravitational pressures do not affect him. Supine he lies, eyes closed, arms spread, looking toward the gray revolving ceiling with an expression simultaneously so profound and joyous that it is all I can do to combat my shame for yielding so easily to what he may transcend.

# 13

Sol is a Class C star, really little larger than a dwarf, now on the cycle of ascendance. It has been estimated by the best astronomers that in five or six billion years Sol will lose all energy, dwindle in size to become a husk, and then explode with the deadly power of an exterminator's tool. Far before then, however, it will have lost the capacity to sustain intelligent life on any of the inner planets; it is quite doubtful, therefore, that this destruction will be witnessed at close hand by many.

The surface temperature of Sol is several million degrees. This is hot enough to warp a spaceship in seconds, to say nothing of a thinly shielded human form.

# 14

"Special treatment," they say, lumbering into the room. "Now we will find out. We will discover why this mission failed."

These are new personnel, heavy, some wearing full-dress uniforms with medals. I go with them unprotestingly; we scuttle through corridors.

"The truth," I say. "That is of as much interest to me as to you. I want to know. I want to know what happened. Please tell me what happened so that then I can tell you. It is simple. It is all before us. If we can but find it."

"Where is the Captain?" the machines ask. They have taken me to machines. Now I sit shielded by copper, my head dwarfed by helmeting, trying to get to the center of the matter. "Why did you kill him?" the machines inquire. "How did the ship turn around?" they query, and "How did you get home alone in a two-man capsule?" and restraints or no I try to tell them—gesture vigorously, use my hands to make a particularly intricate point—but the straps are quite binding and I have to do the best I can with the sole armor of my voice. Which I do not understand.

After a while it stops—machines, voice, restraints, everything—and I am returned to my room. There fresh piles of cryptograms and puzzles await me.

# 15

My wife and I seem to be having an argument. "I hate the program," she says to me. "I can't stand it any more. I want you to leave. If you won't leave, I will, alone, and the hell with your damned public relations. Please, Harry," she says, holding her breasts in her hands. (We are both naked; this discussion is taking place in bed.) "See these? For these do it for me. I know you hate it too. You told me once. For what we had together—"

She seems to feel that I am passionately attracted to her breasts. This is not at all true now, although there was a time when I rather liked them. It must be that time to which she is referring. "I'm not machinery," she is saying. "I'm not programmed. I'm a human being, with wants and desires. Leave, Harry, or I can't tell what may happen to us." She pauses, rolls to one side, but her hands are still holding her breasts and the roll is broken by her elbow. Dramatic posturing is very difficult in bed.

"Remember Mars, Harry," she says.

"Mars was a freak occurrence. It won't happen again."

"It's happening all the time."

"Anyway, I'm not going to Mars. I'm going to Venus."

"You're insane," she says. Her body shakes, the fine curve of her buttocks trembling. "All of you are insane. You can't take this seriously. Not after what's happened. Harry, you have to get out or I will, I swear it. No more, no more."

"We'll see," I say and with a sweeping gesture place a hand on her thighs, roll her back, turn her over, move to enormous height and hover over; begin to fuck her. Insertion is accomplished easily; buccal tendencies are negligible. We have been geared for efficiency. I begin to fuck her like a proper astronaut, hands clamped into fists at her side, the whole body geared to the piston of the prick which is so neatly inserted into its aperture of proper tension. Fluids rise and billow within me; hatches fall on schedule. I come quietly, efficiently, touching no part of her, and remain above, staring at the ceiling.

"Now I mean it, Harry," she says, "I do mean it"; and I ask her what she is talking about, what she means, what she has on her mind, and for reasons which I do not understand, she begins to cry. More and more she has been out of contact recently. It must be that my selection for the Venus mission has overawed her and she no longer knows how to deal with a man of my potential and accomplishments.

# 16

On the ship the Captain proposes that we play a game to pass the time. "We have nothing to do otherwise," he says. "Everything is automated; even the respiration is by machine. We must try to entertain each other or we will break under the stress." I remind him that every word we say to each other inside the capsule is taped for later playback, but the Captain says that this does not matter. "Only if we bugger each other or do something serious. Otherwise, they don't care."

He suggests that each of us in turn asks the other a question to which the other must respond truthfully. The truth must be absolute; there must be no hedging or lying; and the game will continue until each of us either answers three questions satisfactorily or refuses to respond, in which case the person who has asked the question will be the winner. If there is any suspicion of lying, the one under suspicion will have exactly thirty seconds to prove his statement or lose.

Also, each question must be answered in no more than fifty words. "Otherwise things will begin to drag and become sentimental," the Captain says. "There is no truth which cannot be given in fifty words; the truth is always concise. Do you want to play, Evans? I outrank you, you understand, and if you refuse, I will make this trip miserable."

"Why must we?" I say, looking through a porthole, admiring the gray sweep of the heavens almost motionless against the plate, no sensation of travel whatsoever as we continue toward Venus at a rate of fifteen miles per second. Without atmospheric shielding, the stars look like small vacuums torn through the universe. "Couldn't we just concentrate on the mission?"

"There is no mission," the Captain says, rubbing his hands. We have been in transit now for six days and the Captain has been showing clear signs of instability, becoming progressively ominous over the last hours. "The mission is merely a state of mind; an alteration of consciousness. This is nothing but another simulation."

"No, it isn't," I say, "and even if it were, we have no choice. We believe it to be a mission."

"Don't be preposterous, Evans," the Captain says. "I haven't gone mad. Madness has nothing to do with it. We have three hours until the next transmission and code check. Will you play or not?"

"They're listening to us."

"Nobody's listening to us. Don't you realize that, Evans? Nobody cares. We can do anything we want here because only results count. I didn't want you on this mission. When I learned you had finished second in the tests, I did everything within my power as the commander to have you replaced by the next man down. I never liked you, never at all."

"All right," I say, "I'll play." The Captain's disapproval, the hard, rancid lines of his face as they draw into accusation, disconcert me. With all his limitations he is my companion, the only human being within several million miles, in an ambition of unspeakable importance, and I do not want to disappoint him. "Even though I don't know what you want."

"That's excellent," the Captain says. He adjusts himself in his seat, runs his hands through his hair, winks at a porthole, and then turns to me. "Why do you think we're on our way to Venus?" he asks.

"Is that the question you're asking or is that something else?"

"Damn you, Evans," the Captain says, "that's the question. Answer the question."

I lean back, close my eyes, think. The Captain has said nothing about time limits for our preparation of the answers nor for that matter has he suggested any kind of penalties for the loser of the game. After a time he says, "Answer now, Evans. Your time is up."

"I'm still thinking."

"Time has expired."

"You didn't give a time limit."

"I don't have to give a limit. I'm the Captain. I can do anything I damned well please."

"All right," I say, "the reason we're going to Venus, the truthful reason, is that there's an enormous amount of hardware and administrative bureaucracy which must be utilized and is under severe pressure because of the Mars problem. Also, our going will keep people's minds off our international policy. Is that what you wanted to hear?"

"You almost went over fifty words."

"But I didn't. That's the truth."

The Captain sighs, leans back almost luxuriously, puts his arms behind his head, shoves his groin at me. "I'm sorry," he says. "You lose. That is not the truth. And the penalty is that you have got to keep on answering until you either give me the truth or I decide to release you. Try again."

"I can't."

"Try again," the Captain says and takes from his pocket an enormous, contraband nail file which he draws across his fingers in a menacing way. "That's a direct order."

"You didn't tell me the penalty before."

"I didn't have to. I don't have to tell you anything. I'm the Captain and this is my ship and you play by my rules. You may think that I'm going mad, Evans, but you're the one who is being slowly destroyed by the pressures of space; I'm better than I ever was. Answer the question. Answer the question!"

I am about to say that he is being unfair and unreasonable when, interrupting us, there is a sudden disturbance in the ship; an alteration of metal which causes even the interior surfaces to seemingly buckle for an instant. With a great clamor the first, but hardly the last, of the Great Venus Disturbances attacks us, scattering crockery and transmission equipment, while voices from the green planet wordlessly chant in our brains, warning us to stay away.

# 17

Evans, with great intensity, ponders a bridge problem in his room. South has stripped the hands to position play and now holds four hearts to the ace–jack; three small spades and the ace of diamonds in the dummy. He must take all of the remaining tricks at no trump, but West is on the lead and holds the ace–king of spades. "Impossible," Evans murmurs, "impossible," but bridge puzzles, along with anagrams, are of great comfort to him, and he cannot abandon this one so cheaply; if he does, there will be one less element in his life that he can take seriously. He visualizes West, a ponderous man wearing space gear and a helmet, the kind of man who would perhaps never actually land on the moon or Mars but would be steady enough to be left behind in the capsule, whirling in orbit and doing small tasks until the others returned. "Come on," Evans says to West, "you don't really want to lead that spade now, do you? You want to hold back, make an endplay, take the final tricks with your spades after you've set up the side suit. Try a heart. There, that small heart in your hand, right there. Squeeze me out, come now." West smiles, nods, shakes his head, and seems to blush. "Well," he says, "I don't really *know;* I mean I'd like to, but then I don't want to get greedy, and then again—"

"No spades," Evans says again, his voice slightly hoarse with the tension of the hand. He imagines West's capable hands operating the levers of machinery vaulting a seismic device toward the moon or maybe squeezing the life out of some helpless reporter who had questioned the efficacy of the program. He is excited by West; he feels that they can talk man to man. "Listen," Evans says, "don't worry about greed. Play. Play to win. But you really don't want to lead that high spade."

"Ah," West says, "ah, well." He frowns, shakes his head, his face clotted with concentration and doubt. He fumbles amidst the cards in his hands; Evans holds his breath and waits for the play to evolve. He has done the best he can; he has appealed to West's better nature by trying to outwit him. "Besides," Evans murmurs in a tiny voice, just as the card is played, "I'd really like to win this hand; I need the points."

Quivering, face up on the table, Evans sees the ace of spades.

West holds his hand over it like a collaborator, blushing. "I'm sorry," he says with infinite regret. "I'm sorry, I'm sorry, but I'd better take the trick while I can, and the whole world doesn't turn around you, Evans, even though you were almost tops in the program."

With a scream Evans leaps right toward him, right toward West's throat, in an attempt to grab and shake or squeeze the life out of that bland, bobbing face, but before he can quite get hold, the card table explodes; the cards whirl, forming a tube of enormous strength and tensility that penetrates the ceiling; the ceiling parts, the room collapses, the situation dissolves, and with a groan Evans realizes that he has lost yet another brain-twister.

His logical facilities are short; the strain has had an effect upon him and there is no reason for him to be embarrassed; his full mental powers will return when they leave him alone again, but all this rationalization has no effect upon him; he finds that he is wiping his cheekbones with his palms as if they were slate and babbling with shame.

# 18

"Because man must explore," I say to the Captain after the First Great Venus Disturbance has been quelled, the voices of the Venusians stilled in our brains and the alien presences, grumbling, repelled for the moment by our superior will. "Man must forage outward and Venus is our California, our Spain, our moon. We must expand ceaselessly and restlessly because our curiosity and courage are the survival quotient of the race."

"Wrong," the Captain says with a chuckle. "I'm afraid that you really are very poor at this game, Evans. Keep trying. Keep trying, however. We have a week before Venus orbit; maybe you'll get it by then."

# 19

Lush with embarrassment I tell the girl I want her to become my wife. "I'm sure that we can work it out. The program is phasing down anyway."

"You're really dedicated to the program though, aren't you?" she says, permitting me to fondle her breasts from behind. It is some years ago and we are sitting in the back seat of my old convertible on a hill overlooking the town nearest to the project; surprisingly, despite the fact that I am well known in the town and adequately placed within the project, this is the greatest sexual liberty I have ever been able to take with this girl. "I mean, I can see it."

"It's my work," I say, "but not necessarily my life. My life is many things. I want it to be you."

"Yes," she says, placing her hands over mine as if in admonition and then, strangely, drawing them closer, "I know that now, but I really can't get along with this kind of life, I just don't believe in it. I don't even know how I got involved with you; I hate spacemen. You won't leave, will you?"

"Why not?" I say. I am twenty-five years old and somewhat reckless; also, the feeling of her breasts palpitating slowly under my hands, just the suggestion of a nipple, excites me. "Why not?"

"I'm not saying I will or won't marry you unless you get out, but I wouldn't be happy. Not really."

"I could get out."

"I wouldn't force you to leave, but I'd make you miserable; I couldn't help that. Don't go any further; I can't stand it. Don't excite me."

"No," I murmur, "I won't excite you, won't excite you," and draw her against me, put my lips into her neck, teeth into her neck, teeth leaving gentle marks all around her, and closing my eyes, falling against her feel the sounds of her body overtaking me; her body sounds like the inside of a capsule, the wicker of her blood the sound of motors, and perversely aroused I go further and further with her, careless of intention finger her unresisting cunt until she is moist, and then just at the point of captivity hear her say with enormous detachment, "Harry, if you marry me, it will never work out. We don't believe in the same things, not at all, but if you want to get married, I will," and I do not know what seizes me first, the emotion of knowing we are affianced or the flower of my coming, but I am taken by an orgasm right then and hold her helplessly, whimpering, sealing our engagement with a groan as one absent spotlight from the project sweeps past us and cutting through the grass turns to show us the hard shadows of the town as it lies below, receptive.

# 20

"This will not work," a fat nervous man says to me, tapping a pencil on his desk. He sits behind a nameplate indicating that his name is Claude Forrest and that he is a doctor of medicine, clinical neurology. "It is not working at all." He shakes his head, then spits into a wastebasket beside him. "If I didn't understand the syndrome so well I'd say that you were being perverse. I'd say that you were faking it! Faking it, do you hear me!" he shouts, half-rising from his seat and then sitting just as quickly, shaking his head. "But you're not, are you?"

"No," I say. I want to be cooperative with Claude Forrest, clinical neurology, just as I have tried to cooperate with all of the institutional personnel. They are only doing their jobs and I owe them courtesy and restraint. Occasionally they will do stupid things like introducing me to my wife and I will lose my temper, but this is really not my fault and most of the time I try to be reasonable. "Of course not."

"You're so calm," Claude Forrest says. "So *calm*. Deadly, implacable—" He stops, takes out a handkerchief, wipes his forehead. "Excuse me," he says. "We're all under consummate strain here. Caused to no small degree by you."

"I'm sorry."

"Do you realize that hundreds of people, this entire facility, have been mobilized for you? Hundreds of thousands of dollars are being spent to give you the best of care, and in return—"

"I'm truly appreciative," I say. I mean this. I have nothing against the institution; the program has always tried to take care of its own. "You know that."

"What happened?" he says. "Tell me, what happened?"

"What happened where?" I ask mildly, inquiring, curious. "I don't understand what you mean."

"What happened on the *ship?*" Forrest puts the handkerchief away, leans toward me. "This can't go on indefinitely, you know," he points out. "We're going to have to take drastic action. We have as much respect for you as anybody could, but we have to get at the information and we know you have it. It's buried somewhere in that disassociated skull of yours and if you won't yield it routinely, we're going to have to go in and get it, no matter what the cost. Re-enactment therapy has its points and I've been very much in favor of it, but if we have to implode—"

"But you don't have to do that," I say. "There's no need for you to threaten me; I'm perfectly willing to tell you exactly what happened. The Captain and I had a disagreement just as we were

26

settling into orbit and I murdered him. He wanted to skip the telecast because he thought that we should concentrate upon the experiments, and I felt that the telecast was very important and that we owed the world this reassurance. I tried to reason with him, but he became stubborn and pulled his rank on me. Then he said that he had never cared for me anyway and he was going to throw acid in my face. Somewhere he had secreted a vial, which he took from one of the bulkheads and showed me. I became terribly frightened and he started to make gestures as if he would toss it in my face. Pleading with him to stop, to no avail, I took a wrench from one of the cabinets and raised it to show him that I had a weapon; he lost his temper entirely and lunged toward me. I struck him heavily on the temple and he fell in his tracks, the acid spilling harmlessly on the shielding, where it caused almost imperceptible damage. Instantly I became frightened because I felt the fact I had killed him in self-defense might not seem credible, and in any event, all of this would be horribly embarrassing to the program. I entirely lost my calm. Clumsily picking him up, I managed to put him into an evacuation chamber and then discharged him with enough force to hurl him free of the Venus orbit and directly toward the sun. He fell into the sun. That is exactly the way it happened and I hope that I've settled the matter."

"I can't stand it," Forrest says, leaning back in the chair, looking up at the ceiling. "I realize my obligations and from the professional point of view I understand the situation, but—"

"I'm truly sorry," I say. "I see that I can't mislead you any more and it was my mistake. I should have realized that the monitors did not cut out until much later; therefore you have reviewed the tapes and see that I'm lying to you. So I won't try to protect the Captain or the program any more and I'm now willing to tell you the final facts of the matter. The Captain made an unspeakable sexual attack upon me. The rays in space or the pressure of the voyage must have unsettled his mind, and he said that he had always had homosexual impulses and by God now he was going to act on them; if you couldn't do what you wanted to do thirty

27

million miles from earth, when were you going to get to do it? He came toward me and I was so stunned that I just sat there frozen. Just as he came toward me the excitement must have become too much for him: his face suffused and he lost his balance; he fell to his knees and just then the ship pitched in orbit and he rolled straight into the open evacuation capsule, which was filled with fecal wastes that we had been about to discharge, and the pressure of his rolling body pushed him and the capsule out into space, the door closing behind him. I was terribly shocked, of course, but did what I could to repair the situation. I closed the exit hatch and canceled the transmissions; I studied the machinery carefully so that I would be able to give the launch signals and counterbalance my weight in such a way that the path of the return voyage would·be smooth. Up until now I have concealed the truth from you because I have been ashamed; have felt emotions that I could never, until this moment, have admitted.

"I have always had homosexual impulses too. I was no different from the Captain. The space rays made me desirous as well and throughout the voyage I sneaked covert looks at him while he was sleeping; admired the stricken panels of his face and thought of the music of our connection; imagined my hand sliding toward his pubis and the horrified wink of the monitors as, deep within, the tape recorded this scatology as the full and final record of the Venus expedition. I wanted him to touch me as much as he did, but I could not face this and so quailed from him instead, causing this unfortunate accident. I am sorry I held this back so long, but you can imagine how embarrassed I've been about all this and how bad the publicity would be if word got around that your astronauts on the first trip to Venus had nothing more inspiring going through their heads than buggering one another."

". . . drastic actions," Forrest is saying. "I am warning you for the last time, Evans. If this does not stop, we will have to take actions so drastic that your mind will be ruined. You will be a pulp and you will live in a tube for the rest of your life, sucking fluids and looking at the ceiling of this institution. We will have to do it. The stakes are too large—"

"I'm convinced," I say. "I don't want to live in a tube; I want to see the sun again, to receive a commendation from the President, and someday even to remarry. Because you will agree, I really can't live with this particular woman any more; we never got along. So let me confess: let me tell you. Venus, it turns out, is populated by an intelligent race of malevolent green snakes. I couldn't tell you this before because they shrouded my mind with their beams, but now the conditioning is beginning to wear off and they are no longer protected. We are far more resistant than they would think and I can shake off the conditioning, as I am doing now. They detected our coming through force screens and radar devices and communicated telepathically with us through voices in our heads. They said that language did not matter because they were transmitting emotion through the hypothalamus; and we were to turn around and go home or otherwise we would be destroyed because Venus was entitled to their secrecy and their independence; and the last time people from our planet had come out toward them, thousands of years ago, they had gotten into real trouble. They became very threatening and abusive and made pictures in our heads showing exactly what could happen to us if we didn't turn around and I became very frightened. I was all for giving up. But of course we couldn't turn around because we had no way of controlling the ship at all; everything was on remote without an override and we would have looked pretty ridiculous and insane trying to explain through the transmissions that intelligent green Venusian snakes were controlling our minds. The Captain knew we couldn't turn around, but he didn't say that; he became very stubborn and abusive and said that no goddamned foreign bastard of a Venusian was going to tell him what to do, and then he said that we had atomic devices aboard which could incinerate their whole planet if they didn't leave well enough alone. I don't know whether their telepathy was two-way

29

so that they could tell what was in his mind as well as they could project or whether they knew that that was a lie, but they became very angry and said that in that event they were no longer going to treat us as if we were civilized beings. They said they were going to do something to the Captain's pineal gland to make him go crazy and commit suicide, and I could watch the whole thing happen and then go back and report to Earth what their powers were so they wouldn't be bothered again. So they did something to his pineal and he walked right into the capsule and ejected himself and then they told me to get back and give that message, but because of the shock of the conditioning, I couldn't do it until right now. But I've just recovered my memory and that's the fact of the matter. Is that all right? I had to protect the Captain's reputation anyway, you see: I couldn't let just anyone know how stupid he had been."

"The ship did have atomic devices, you know," Forrest says quietly. "That part is true."

"Oh?"

"That has been standard procedure on these flights for a long time. The Pentagon wants us to carry fusion bombs, so we do. Of course, this is knowledge given only to the commander. The devices are in a shielded bulkhead invulnerable to penetration, with the emergency trigger well concealed, and there's no reason why the second man in the capsule should have any such knowledge. So that is very interesting."

"Oh," I say, "I forgot to tell you. I mean I lied to you the first time around and now I can't bear to lie any more because I see how crucial the information is. The Captain never said anything about having nuclear devices. They said, 'Do you have any weapons on board?' and he said, 'No, we come in the friendliest spirit of exploration,' and they said, 'In that event, since you will be unable to protect yourselves, we can carry on our loathsome acts without fear of retaliation.' I made up the part about his saying we have explosives. I made up all of it."

Forrest puts his hands across the desk, shows them to me:

squat little fingers, out of proportion to the large palms, damp with nicotine and the color of the sun. "You've had your last warning, Evans," he says, "and I don't believe that you're incapable of telling what you know. There are some here who hold to that view, but I am senior and I've never paid it much credence. You are perfectly oriented for time, place, and person; you are completely lucid and know exactly what you're doing. Do you see these hands?" he says and opens the palms, turns them toward me, shows me creases like scars on the face of the moon. "These hands," Forrest says, "these *hands* are going to burn it out of you. Burn it out of you, you son of a bitch, because it's the only way. So think about it. Go back to your bulkheads and think about it and then—"

"I will," I say hastily. "I've already thought about it and believe me, you're right; it isn't worth it. The truth will out, it cannot be held back any longer, and the price I will have to pay is not worth what is being asked, particularly since the Captain is now dead and I no longer need to shield a living man but only a reputation. So let me tell you that he was a pederast and—"

But arms have gripped me strongly from behind—why was I not aware of attendants?—and I feel a sensation of speed: I am being dragged from the room at great speed, am being turned in those arms like a capsule, the floor spinning underneath me like pale, fair Venus grinning so bleakly at our humble ship the first time we settled around her.

# 21

The moon is the single satellite of our planet, approximately one quarter of our space and volume, which led both ancient and modern astronomers to many interesting speculations. With the possible exception of Triton, lone moon of Neptune, no other single satellite exists in our system; but most new research indicates that Pluto is not a planet but also a moon of Neptune, thereby leaving ours alone as a single satellite.

Since all of the other moons are also in much less proportion to their planets than our moon to earth, theories have been advanced that we do not have a satellite system at all but a dual planet: one dead, one alive; one possibly captured by the orbit of the other inconceivable eons ago in an enormous nuclear disaster. Despite the hopes held out by the manned expeditions to the moon, now abandoned, no firm data were ever uncovered to either confirm or destroy this theory.

Men first landed on the moon in 1969. They returned in 1970, 1971, 1972, and 1973 for progressively longer missions. The program was then abandoned, having been in a process of phase-out for many years before that, because in the difficult political atmosphere of those times the economy of the United States, which was responsible for all the moon landings, would no longer support the moon program. In 1975, however, the program was fully revived toward the crash priority of a landing on Mars in 1976, the next favorable conjunction of the earth and Mars. A Venus expedition occurred in 1981 and plans existed for a series of expeditions to Venus, followed by voyages to the outer planets and finally, in the year 2000, to Mercury.

The moon, however, was abandoned, and except for certain discarded articles of clothing and machinery, certain slight alterations in its orbit caused by the explosion of nuclear devices, no significant indication of man's presence remains.

Similarly, no trace of men exists on Mars, one of the reasons for this being that men never got there.

In 1981, however, men conquered Venus and a new area of exploration began.

# 22

"We went to Venus," I say to the Captain, "because our minds were really controlled by Venusians who wanted to lure us there and then kill us. The Venusians are a far more advanced race than we, and very cunning; what we took for our own independent actions were really theirs. That is why we went to Venus."

"No," the Captain says, opening his book of logarithms and making a note on the table of contents. "That is not true. Still, I admire your persistence, Evans, and if you stay with it I'm sure that you'll come up with something sooner or later. Ignore the sounds in our heads; concentrate on the game and all will eventually come clear."

"When does my turn come?" I ask. "When will I be able to put a question to you? I have several in mind."

"First you must answer mine and then the turn passes. You cannot ask until you have been successful."

"But that may never happen!"

"I'm sorry, Evans," the Captain says resignedly. "Those are the rules of the game. Of course, the senior in command has the right to ask the first question, and as you can see, I'm being perfectly fair."

"Well then," I say, trying again, "in that case, the real reason we are going to Venus—"

But the ship begins to shake in earnest then, the second of the Great Venus Disturbances obviously beginning, and for some time I am not able to say anything at all.

# 23

It is time for me to make an anagram of my name. Perhaps this will lead me more densely into the mystery. The doors are locked now and I have lost hall and bathroom privileges; it is more and more difficult to remain happily absorbed within this small room, and so I must investigate every device carefully, try to find pleasure and meaning in the simplest explorations. EVANS.

SAVEN

NAVES

SNAVE

VANES

VASEN

VENAS

The Captain appears beside me suddenly, infinitely wise, infinitely pained. *"Senav,"* he says, "you forgot *Senav.* That is an anagram of Evans and a very good one too. Senav was my mother's maiden name. Lila Senav. Of course that was a long time ago. I haven't seen my mother for a decade. She's dead, you know. Lila Senav is dead."

He winks at me, compelling, gratuitous, in the dim spaces of my locked room. "We've both come a long way, haven't we, Evans?" he says and regretfully vanishes.

# 24

I had small flashes of impotence with my wife, beginning when I passed all the tests and found that I had come second on the Venus program; was due for heavy training and embarkation within six months. First it was a matter of coming too fast; then when I used an old technique I had read once in a sex manual and closed my eyes while fucking to think of neutral things, I found that my mind was stuck on machinery—the gearing of the space-craft, on which I was an expert—and I was unable to unload. My prick would get soft within her, locked to detumescence, and no matter how I tried to bring my mind back to the business of fuck-ing, I could not progress. For a while we made no mention of it, since sex had not been that important in our marriage for a long time, but finally my wife suggested that I seek some kind of help. "The place is lousy with psychiatrists," she said. "They monitor every breath you take. Don't you think you should talk to them about this problem? They might be able to give you a prescrip-tion."

"It's nothing," I said, embarrassed. I had thought so little of her sexual responses that until she brought up the matter, I was not sure that she had noticed. "Just a little bit of tension, that's all."

"It's been going on for weeks. Ever since you found out you were going to Venus. I think the two are connected."

"It doesn't mean a thing," I said. "I've just been preoccu-pied, knowing what's ahead of me. Look, it's ready to work now." I pointed down at my organ, which indeed was in genuine erection, poised and ready to enter her as we lay side by side, not touching, on the bed, she with a ladies' magazine and me holding some gravitational reports across my stomach. "I'll do it right now," I said, and before I could think about it further, move into complications of resistance, leaned over, pivoted on an elbow, lifted her nightgown and mounted her. She lay there, holding the magazine, staring at the ceiling.

"I don't like the publicity," she said as I fucked her. "This rag wants to interview me. I don't want to be interviewed."

"So don't," I said, humping away, my eye caught by an illustration showing an attractive housewife holding a kitchen implement shaped like a rocket, using it to perform an apparently grotesque act upon a cake nearby. "Don't be interviewed," I said, swinging my head between housewife and laid wife under me, feeling my semen rise expertly within the various tubes and layers underneath. "They can't take away your privacy," and I felt my breath contract, my lungs wheeze, my eyes clot, while I quite easily deposited into her or the housewife, it being difficult to tell between the two at the moment of coming, a considerable amount of sperm. Almost immediately I felt shame as she absently dabbed at the spot with a fist, forcing me out of her, flapping the magazine and then laying it by the bedside, taking off her glasses and folding them with a click, then rolling to one side, toppling me, and pounding her hand into the pillow.

"Good night," she said.

"Is that all?"

"What else? I heard from one of your administrators today. He thinks it would be a really good idea if I cooperated some with the press. 'It would pave the way to Venus' is how he put it. I hung up on him. I'm not cooperating with anyone."

"All right," I said. "Don't. Don't cooperate. It doesn't matter. Can you just turn away from me like that? Just like that and go to sleep?"

"I'm tired. I have nothing more to say."

"There are things on my mind too."

"I know there are, Harry. There are things on everybody's mind. Please, Harry. Please. Don't sound like the man who talked to me today. Don't make me say that all of you sound alike."

"All right," I said, "all right," and turned from her then, met her disinclination with withdrawal of my own; turned to face the wall, hearing her breathing and shifting behind me, small breaths that sounded like moans, all of it dead cold and sterile in the kindly night.

# 25

The novel I will write about the ultimate truth of the voyage will be divided into small chapters, each of which will recapture some aspect of my past or present life, some part of the Captain or the program. I will use the short-chapter format because I do not have the patience for long chapters and because I believe that what happened can be indicated only in small flashes of light, tiny apertures which, like periscopes, will illuminate some speck of an overall situation so large that none of us can comprehend it. Parts of it will be true and some of it will be only as I conceive it, but in totality it will make the final statement about the Venus program and about myself. I must get to this soon. I cannot put it off indefinitely. One must seize the moment. By tomorrow or at the very least by the day after that I will get started. They will not burn my brain for recovery of the information. It is an idle threat, invented by the neurologist Forrest and emerging only from his own despair. I am, or at least was until very recently, the second most qualified man in the program. I have certain rights and recourses even in this situation.

The novel will be brilliant and everyone will want to read it. It will possess great sensitivity and perception and a luminescent sense of structure quivering like roots beneath its incidents. Once and for all it will prove that astronauts are not insensitive mechanical men but people possessed of vast depth and artistic capability who have been ill-used by administrators and are in receipt of poor public relations. All of the works to date by astronauts have been ghostwritten, but the novel I will write will be my own work from first to last because only I can understand and convey the essential sense of mystery which is so crucial. He did not have proper respect.

I loved the Captain. I was devoted to him. His tragic outcome left me shaken but determined to memorialize him in the truest and most essential senses. I loved the Captain. I cannot yet remember his name, but soon enough it will come to me and then the last piece of the portrait will fit. He did not have proper respect, but I had never held this against him.

# 26

Evans thinks he hears his wife in the corridors, prowling outside his locked door, pressing her occasional ear against steel, trying to hear his sounds. This is the kind of thing that they would do; he expects nothing else from them. Nothing. They would convey his wife to the institution and order her to extract information; if she was unsuccessful that way they would give her provisions and leave her to spy in the night. Despite their helplessness they are cunning, ruthless. Through the thin walls Evans thinks that he can hear footsteps, business, breaths. "I know you're out there," he says, putting a chess puzzle from him. "I know it, I know it: you can't delude me, I've been to Venus."

He stands, moves to the door, tries once again to open it, but it is locked. He fits his mouth instead against the panels like a kiss.

"It makes no difference," he says to his wife, who is surely outside listening attentively to him, her fine, wide body sprung like a bow against the knob, her hand clutching a cheek in characteristic posture, her eyes dull and moistening now to the impact of his words. "I know you're out there, you see, but you will obtain nothing from me. Go home. Go home. Leave the project. You are free now."

"You see," Evans says conversationally to his listening wife, willing to explain further, "I wanted to change lives. I wanted to alter circumstances. I wanted them to see that what they were living was only one small fragment, an alternative, really, to many other lives; that we had selected the smallest particle of possible experiences and called it the only one. I tried to show them that; I tried to make it through the Captain. The Captain was the key and now he is gone. I'm sorry," Evans says, wrapping it up because he has really said all that is on his mind, "but that's all that I can say to you. You can go home now. I'm going to sleep. Conversation will stop."

He listens for his wife's response, but there is no response; a contraction of lights in his room, a slight quaking at the center of the institutional maintenance machinery, that is all . . . no indication whatsoever that she has heard him or she will change. "You must change," Evans says, "you must; we can never live from here on in the way it was in the past," and he hears footsteps. Yes, the footsteps are diminishing, his wife is going away from him, all of them are going away from him, and Evans, still leaning against the door, finds that he has a few last words to say; he talks ceaselessly into the door, into the night, willing at last to tell them what he has done and is trying to do, but except for the stenographic rumble of the machines there is no sound at all, and finally Evans, from boredom, stops. He is sick of the sound of his own voice. For all these weeks and months he has heard nothing else: the rising and falling, the mumbling and complaining of his own voice sounding teeny-tiny in his skull, not to be canceled out by examinations, procedures, cryptograms, or interviews, and now at last there is time to quit. He will talk no more. This night he will say nothing else. Evans, of whom not enough can be said, walks quietly to his bed in the gloom and sits on it in stillness, hands against his ears, pondering, but as hard as he clamps, as desperately as he squeezes, he still cannot shut off the sound of his voice, which goes on and on, open and modulating, high-pitched and lean, through all the spaces to dawn.

# 27

"Turn back," the voices creating the Third Great Venusian Disturbance say, "turn back before it's too late. Backwards, earthmen, backwards turn time in thy flight. Abandon the mission. Abort your controls. This is our last warning."

"I'm truly sorry," the Captain says regretfully. As senior in command he, of course, addresses the voices of the Disturbance while Evans sits by respectfully, awaiting further direction. "There's no way that we can do that. The mission is on complete automatic. We are merely passengers."

"Lies," the voices say, curiously monomaniacal. As forceful as the Venusians appear to be they are also curiously limited, obsessed, imperceptive to reason. "All of these are lies and propaganda. Back, earthmen. Turn back."

"But you really don't understand," the Captain says. "We don't operate these craft at all. We're baggage. The only reason we're here is to give the illusion of control. It's all happening back at the base, millions and millions of miles from here, and I don't suppose you could reach them, could you? Go ahead and talk to them; we'll cooperate. No, I guess you couldn't."

"Do not interfere with Venus. Venus is the planet of remorse and solitude. Back, back."

"We would if we could," the Captain says. "Isn't that true, Evans? Tell them that we'd be perfectly willing to abort if we were able, but it isn't possible."

"Oh, yes," Evans says. "Definitely. If we had known that your planet was inhabited or that you wouldn't be happy with this mission we never would have come. And we'd gladly turn around if we could. Of course. Surely."

"Evans is the second in command," the Captain says. "He's here to monitor my reactions and every now and then I check on his. That way they make sure that nobody gets away with anything like pissing into the microphones. Tell them, Evans."

"Yes, that's true."

"He'll confirm everything I'm saying. The ship is out of our hands."

"That's absolutely true," Evans agrees. A touch of obsequity enters his voice; he has always, although he denied this, wanted the approval of superior individuals or institutions. "The Captain is the most qualified man on our planet and he wouldn't mislead you. I'm only the second in command."

"Enough of these sophistries," the Venusian says and creates a sudden and horrid blaze of color inside Evans' head. "We are quite out of patience. Unless you cooperate, we will have to take drastic action."

"That's too bad," the Captain says quietly. "We've told you the truth."

"You are not hallucinating. Every instant of this dialogue is real. We are speaking to you from a distance of thirty million miles, but we exist."

"I wouldn't doubt that," the Captain says. "Not for a moment." He stands, moves around the small area of the capsule, his hands clenched, touching machinery purposefully. "But you see, there's nothing we can do."

"Enough," the voice says, "enough!" and caresses certain

ganglia, dislocates tendons, causes one jarring burst of pain as it withdraws, leaving us shaken and alone in the capsule. Alone, of course, we always were. The Captain shrugs delicately and runs a finger across his teeth, then sits. "They'll never believe any of this," he says. "There's no way that we can convince them. I suggest that we say nothing about it."

"That's all right with me," Evans says. He has no complement to the Captain's teeth-touching gesture but performs certain small nervous mannerisms of his own: familiar tugs, pinches, pulls, to realign himself in a more military direction. "I wouldn't say a word about it."

"That's good," the Captain says. He pauses, looks at the ceiling, stretches his legs. Unbidden, a small tune seems to burst from him; he hums quietly, he whistles. He shrugs. "Well," he says, "do you want to get back to the game?"

"All right," Evans says. He is afflicted by the same reaction which the Captain feels: a certain dislocation, a clear detachment. The Great Venus Disturbance certainly has complicated the voyage, but since there is no room for it in the scheduling, there is no sense in worrying about it. The Venusians are out of his hands, along with the ship and the mission. "The reason we're going to Venus is that the administration knows there are Venusians and they hope to precipitate an interplanetary war which will draw the nations of earth close together against a common enemy as the only means of survival. The psychologists figured it out and the administrators went along."

"You mean," the Captain says, "as I understand this, that humanity can only join together against a common foe and the Venusians will group all of mankind against them."

"Exactly," I say, "is that right? Did I answer?"

"That's an old science-fiction theme, you know," the Captain says. He seems poised, judicious, in the aftermath of the Venusians' warning; more positive and assertive than I have seen him since the times in the training center. He examines his nails again and drums one hand against the other. "I never had much use for science fiction."

"I never did either."

"It gave the program a bad name, science fiction did. It was so disreputable in the minds of most people that the program had to be as businesslike as possible in order to seem legitimate. Perhaps we became a little stuffy," the Captain says, "as I think about it."

"That's a good point."

"But then again it's hard to say; maybe the program was put together by people who believed in science fiction and this is the way all science-fiction characters acted."

"That's true too," I say agreeably. It is strange: the Captain and I are now having a relaxed and civilized discussion millions of miles from earth while Venusians threaten to destroy us. It seems wholly natural, wholly credible, and any moment I expect small aphorisms and whimsies, yarns and anecdotes to be exchanged.

"We'll have to discuss that further," the Captain says. "Meanwhile, I have to say that you're wrong. The Venusians have nothing to do with it. The administrators didn't even know that there were such things as Venusians. I'm the commander, they gave me all the private and detailed information, and they never expected that at all. So you have to guess again."

"Don't you think we should do something else?" I say. "Try to figure out a way to protect ourselves against the attack, or turn the ship around and head back without letting them know what's happened, or maybe think up a way to reason with these aliens so that they'll see our point? Wouldn't that be more profitable than doing this?"

"No," the Captain says and yawns. "It wouldn't make any difference whatsoever. We're going to do exactly what we're doing and it will work out the same way, whether or not. No matter the difference. We have nothing else to do with this. So keep on, keep on; you're taking too much time. Surely you want to ask me a question, don't you?"

"Yes," I say, "I want to know about your sex life. If you were ever impotent or if you think that somehow being an astronaut fucked you up inside so you weren't a normal human being in bed. I really would like to know that."

"Well," the Captain says with an amiable grin, "you answer your part of the game and I'll be perfectly happy to tell you the whole truth about that. I really will. But fair's fair, and I'm afraid we can't break the rules."

"No," I say and begin to ponder while the ship contorts; I hear the fluids in the motors pumping like blood, the sounds of the ship becoming abrupt and disturbing; I wonder if we are ready for yet another attack but realize that it is only my eagerness to learn of the Captain's secret sex life which has so attuned my senses, and if I want to learn the answer, I will have to control my excitement and go by the rules. His rules. The ship lurches toward Venus and I prepare another answer.

# 28

In the night I have a dream and this is the most vivid dream of all: Forrest's brain-burning technique must have begun, my brain is being turned outside in; eviscerated, my past is beginning to fall through my consciousness like hunks of ripe meat, swelling on the butcher's hook. In the dream I am fucking my wife, skillfully, expertly, with emotion and persistence; fucking her in all the ways that I never thought I could: emotion and skill and lust are combined in a careful, audacious package and she is loving it, taking all that I can give her and thrusting back at me vigorously. Her eyes are closed, arms above her head, hands clasped behind her neck so that her breasts, hard to their core, are raised toward me, bobbling in response; and every now and then I lean down, not interrupting my pumping motions, to give the breasts a vigorous suck or three, but the sucking is not what interests me—it is merely a courtesy, so to speak, to her arousal—the primary thing is fucking; and in addition to that, when I work on her breasts I cannot talk and it seems I am talking to her inexhaustibly: the sound of my voice richly and floridly filling the room and all the interstices of sex. This is sex as I have never known it, sex as I have never thought it could be; it is not only lust and passion but pedagogy, for in the dream I am lecturing her as I fuck and she is attuned to every word, as attuned to what I have to say to her as to the rich wet connection below, and I give her one and the other together while she nods her head in quick little yanks and occasionally says *yes. Yes, yes. Yes, yes, that's true.*

"Consider repression," I am saying, "consider what they are doing to us: working us over like dogs in their exercises, locking us up for days at a time in their caves so that they can run their tortures, administering programs and patterns of response so that we can have absolutely nothing to do with the running of this craft but to withstand it. Calculating our posture and our speech to the last degree, running reversal tests to make us vomit and testing our pain thresholds so that we shriek, but nevertheless," I say, winging away at her, "*nevertheless* and despite everything that they do to us, I retain my individuality. My pride, my insight, my self-sufficiency. I am still a person; even if I am going to go to Venus I'm still what I always was because there is a core in man which is basic and which cannot be annealed by any of them and I have it, I have it, I still have it."

"Yes," she murmurs, fluttering her eyes at me, her mouth distending into response or agony, it is hard to tell which, "that is absolutely true, but can't you come?" and I realize she is right: she does indeed have a point there, although the dream distorts chronology at the edges and also seems to telescope time, it seems that I have been fucking her for a very long time, perhaps half an hour in the same rhythm, and am no closer to coming than I was at the time of insertion. My skin distends with desire, my prick is as hard and surging as a rocket, but there is no movement outward, no descent into orgasm, and I say, "All right then, bitch, you want me to come, then I'll come," and in my mind depress certain levers and indicators, open up pressure points all up and down the line, command valve locks to retract, and urge from the most hidden part of me my come to ooze forth like blood . . . but it is not easy: something that they have done to us in the gravity simulators (or maybe again it was the centrifugal force orbit simulator into which we were placed) has fucked up my machinery and I am unable to come upon command as I always was before; I am in fact unable to come at all, the levers jam at a crucial instant, the pressure points allow backfill, and suspended above her, my eyes now closed, squeezed against the come that is not there, I begin to feel embarrassment: this after all is not part of the pedagogic intention which underlies this fuck, but on the other hand I can hardly withdraw, not with her working against me so industriously, looking at me doubtless with such growing contempt, so I return as best I can to the tasks under me, opening my eyes to find that she is not looking at me but at the wall, closing my eyes to find that the pictures are not of her, not of women, not even of machinery (an old gambit), but instead of the Captain—hard and proud in his uniform, sitting beside me at a briefing—and it is the image of the Captain more than anything else which touches me off: unbidden it has come to my mind and unbidden I come to it, depositing my load somewhere between his lapels, groaning and screaming, writhing and muttering, shamed in the sudden concentration of my need but satisfied as well, because for all my wife knows I have come into her and not the Captain; she could not tell the difference. We have the integrity of our own heads.

Sensors clipped to my head at this moment might graph out responses dealing with the Captain, but I am on free time; we have been permitted the long weekend with our spouses or families and there is no way that they can get at me. None of them can get at me; this will be my secret forever. The come lasts for a long time, attenuates into a long, heaving space in which it seems that I have somehow gotten deep into her and caused her to erupt as well; but this does not interest me so much as the sheer scattering of my seed, and I withdraw only much later and reluctantly, when I have become too shrunken to persist. "Do you see?" I point out (I forgot to say that I have been talking all through this as well, although my screams and mumbles have perhaps made me incoherent, my pedagogy disguised as simple, grunting passion), "it's the same, it's always the same: you were wrong to say that they would change me because I can do it as well as ever. Can't I? Can't I?" My wife says nothing, I continue to question her, she will not answer, I press her more ferociously, I hear nothing from her, I open my eyes and find that she is gone, the bed is gone, our room is gone, and what I have been doing for the last three quarters of an hour is very industriously if bloodlessly fucking my pillow, which seems to have worked its way down to stomach or thigh level. I look for stains but there are none and then I remember the truth again and for the first time since I have come to this part of my life I quite lose my control and begin to cry but do it deep into the sheets so that no one can hear me, no one can see; and despite what they hint I do not think that there are monitoring devices here or if there are that they can see in the dark; shadows of fluorescence would mark me only as locked deep into the bed, talking with myself about this or that (possibly a cryptogram) until dawn overtakes.

# 29

The Captain comes into the room almost jauntily, as he has been tending to recently, and says, "How are you doing?" his

47

face wrinkling with concentration as he forms the words; then, before I can respond, he has already turned and with some restlessness is looking at the walls, the floor, the piles of puzzles on my bed. "You look a bit confined," he says, "are they giving you a hard time?" and again I ready myself to answer, but the Captain is peripatetic (perhaps his experiences have given him the Long View, made him realize the futility of simple answers to easy questions) and he is once again scurrying around the room, now admiring an old religious engraving hung on one of the walls, now flipping open a desk drawer and examining small fetid piles of my underwear that I have carefully secreted there against the laundering process. "You don't look so good to me, Evans; not at all," he says and wanders to the door. He stands there, drumming his rather insubstantial fingers on the paneling and examining the ceiling, winking and exhaling with astonishment as he notes the extremely poor repair in which the room is kept. "Well, if they're giving you a hard time, just tell them to come to me and I'll straighten them out." He has a slight suntan, his face glazed by heat and concentration, but he is still, as always, extremely handsome and looks far more competent than I to deal with the circumstances with which I am surrounded. "If I can do anything, let me know; I'll be in touch now and then," he says and diminishes through the door, not so much exiting from it as expectorating the scene from his view and leaving me wordless on the bed. There is so much I wanted to ask him but was never given the chance. I have always identified strongly with the Captain. Somehow I believe that there still exists in him the capacity to solve the situation at a stroke if he would, but his mood, rather jocular and distracted as it has been, leaves me without options.

"I'm fine," I say, sitting on the bed. "Everything is all right. They are treating me well, although now they are making threats. My health is fair, with a neurasthenic overlay which disturbs me only at night and during periods of high concentration. I feel neutered sexually. My digestion gives me slight trouble but nothing for which I cannot compensate. All is well," I say, "all is well; come back and let me tell you how I have succeeded," but the Captain does not come back, eager though I may be to talk with him, and after a while I realize that he is merely tantalizing me with his presence—as once and again he must have tantalized his wife with the most delicate of insertions of his prick—and so I return to my contemplations, although there is a hard and rather uneasy edge to them: a frantic scurrying at the root of the brain, which may only be apprehension and then again may be signatory of the fact that Forrest's devices have already been implanted and they are beginning, they are beginning, they are beginning to work.

# 30

At nine the next morning, accompanied by guards, Evans is brought into the presence of Claude Forrest, the most highly placed of all the administrative personnel with whom Evans has dealt. As astronauts go, Evans is a small man—five feet ten or eleven, perhaps—with a physique gone only slightly toward corruption because of his recent difficulties and with large, intense, penetrating eyes that sit in the center of his face, perched like large buttons above the cheekbones, and regard everything with their sad and annealing expression. The eyes take in everything; they have, as the eyes of astronauts must, the look of eagles and have always been the best feature of Evans' face, although the remainder of his face is not to be placed in disrepute as well. Evans has a remarkable face. It is the face of a very handsome man: haunted now by tremors and difficult cryptograms, but nevertheless retaining the hard, incisive blending of personality and integrity which made him so successful throughout his life. It is a face far more attractive than many might think; with a face such as this Evans could have done much better than that bitch he got for a wife—not that he would allow such ungiving thoughts to distract him as, the guards withdrawing, he sits before Forrest in the room.

He sits easily, almost jauntily, scuffling for a cigarette or similar relaxant in his pockets but finds nothing and, slightly disconcerted, turns back to face Forrest, a slight pulse twitching in his cheek. He immediately grasps hold of himself, gives himself a mental shake, and orders the cheek to stop twitching; the weakness subsides, leaving the handsome, passionate, suffering face of Evans quite blank and controlled before the loathsome and inferior Forrest, who looks at him with confusion, sensing Evans' complete and timeless superiority to all of the Forrests of this world, yet condemned to act out a role of social control for his own sick, businesslike reasons. What contempt Evans has for Forrest! How much better he knows of all that has happened than that unfortunate limited man. Even as he thinks of this, he allows a small smile of knowledge to pass across his face, and Forrest jumps in response, completely disconcerted by the control of his adversary, and then seems to settle somewhat lower behind his desk with a dull plop. "Your latest and your last chance, Colonel," he says, "to tell us what happened."

When he hears the word *colonel* used for the first time in their relationship Evans twitches slightly but regains control of himself. Nothing will shake Evans' composure. He is totally in control of himself: a machine. Only in his dreams will he yield and then to himself alone. "Don't call me colonel," he says quietly. "I don't like the grade."

"Why not?"

"That's none of your business," Evans says, leaning across the desk and aiming the words one by one into the pasty neck, the thin, spreading mouth of his enemy. "Nothing is any of your business, Forrest. I repudiate you. I am no longer willing to be polite. I will tell you what I think of all the Forrests of this world;

I think *nothing*," and so on and so forth while Forrest, quite help-less, allows this to wash over him, knowing that the only way in which he can counter righteousness is with a blandness of affect; finally, when Evans has quite talked himself out (my grasp of this scene is somewhat blurred and ragged toward the center; I am able to apprehend it only in a series of snapshots, still lifes, and fast takes of conversation, as it were, and when with heightened concentration I try to move in closer, everything seems to move away from me; perhaps I am somewhat overinvolved with this), Forrest lights a cigarette tantalizingly close to the courageous Evans, takes a puff on it, and says, "That's quite enough, you un-derstand. We are commencing treatments immediately."

"I do not care," Evans seems to say. "There is a higher jus-tice."

"I have tried everything a fair man could. You have no idea of the pressures which have been brought upon me to take this step much earlier. Nevertheless, I fought them off. I did every-thing I could for you and then some."

"Calumny. Calumny in high places. It will not work. Your slender cartoon called reality cannot be compromised with the truth, which only I understand. Why don't you give me a ciga-rette?"

"I will not give you a cigarette," Forrest says and leans back, inhales smoke, divests himself of it with an expirative sigh. "On the other hand, perhaps I will. Why not? If you offer to cooper-ate."

"I have cooperated from the first."

"I'm sorry," Forrest says, a strange, distorted winsomeness coming over his features. "I'm truly sorry about this. We had no choice. I know the price of pain. I know it well. Neverthe-less . . ."

The attendants seem to circle nearer Evans; two grasp him, each by an elbow. The third remains in the background on the possibility of administering a devastating kick to the helpless, handsome spaceman, who nevertheless meets this, as everything, with courage. "I don't care," the heroic spaceman says. "You can do anything to me you want. I have told the truth. My conscience is clear."

"Take him," Forrest says, "take him now," and the scene closes off; everything is quite hidden by the broad and effective backs of the attendants, who block the camera eye, closing me off from the sense of the scene—there is only a funneling of shapes, a blankness of vision—and when all wipes clear I am looking at Forrest alone in the empty room: feet now on the desk, eyes inverted toward the ceiling, sighing and muttering to himself. I lean forward to catch the highly confidential words of Forrest which will enable me to see (possibly for the first time) exactly what this strange and malevolent man has on his mind, precisely how he can rationalize his position to himself, but the words are in a language I do not understand and I cannot apprehend them. "Loksvy termarind," Forrest says, "glou incrabular mock," and I lean closer, determined to force the words past hearing and into the speech-comprehension paths of the brain, but I cannot; he is saying what he is saying and the secret passes. "Momab," Forrest says. "Momab," and as if with a curse, shakes his head, stands, brushes lint off his trousers, and abruptly leaves the room, leaving me in silence and emptiness, to peruse the pages left on his desk if I will (which tell me nothing), to examine his laminated degrees on the wall if I desire (which yield nothing), to consider the small damp traces which Evans' boots have left upon the floor, as some part of him which will reveal what has been going on. But tell me nothing—the spot will tell me nothing—and after a time I leave the room as well, now only the music of the machinery overtaking the spaces and filling them with the sound of craft whirling suspended in orbit.

# 31

The Captain's name was Joseph Jackson. Or Jack Josephson. That much has come back to me: I am sure of it. He was six feet two inches tall and weighed one hundred and eighty-seven pounds. He was thirty-four years old and had been, until the age of twenty-eight when he enlisted in the program, a career officer in the Orbital Laboratory program. Once he entered the program, however, he put all thoughts of the moon behind him and concentrated on the essential task of Venus. Mars he did not think of at all, seeing no point in that. He had a small mole near but not in his left armpit and for twelve years had been married to the same childless woman. He was interested in sports, although in no serious manner, and was totally dedicated to the aim of the program, which was to place a man upon the surface of Venus by the summer of 1981. I remember this clearly now. His wife was tall and well-built and in all ways a satisfying and vigorous fuck—which is more than I can say about my own life, but then I have always had, as was pointed out to me, a tendency to take these things too seriously, which right up to Venus caused me to miss certain aspects of living which later I was able to supersede. Joseph Jackson. Or Jack Josephson. I remember; I remember. Is this my own strengthened recollection, or has Forrest a treatment and is it beginning to work?

# 32

On June 9, 1981, while Jack Josephson and Harry M. Evans were having lunch together in the commissary, seven weeks before their planned launch and in the midst of final training exercises, Joseph Jackson, the commander of the expedition, said, "This will never work. I am positive of this." He whispered these words harshly while holding a small spoon in his hand and delicately conveying fruit cocktail toward his half-opened mouth, and his mouth closed around the fruit in the aftermath of what he had said as if they were all knowledge. "So be it," he said. "So be it."

"Why?" Evans said, working on his own modest lunch, as always being casual and yet deferential with the Captain. Despite the fact that they will voyage and are training together, Evans has not yet worked out a proper attitude toward the Captain. It seems that he should be informal, but on the other hand, the program is founded upon a strict manual of procedures and the Captain is careful of his prerogatives. Also, they had absolutely no contact with each other throughout the program until the selection for the voyage. It was an unpleasant and jarring surprise to Josephson, Evans surmises, when Jackson learned that Evans would be his copilot. He had had other plans or possibly had contemplated a solitary and magnificent voyage in all the spaces of the capsule. "Why is that?"

"Because," Jackson said, and wiped a napkin over his lips with an air of finished business, "I have gone over the figures. I have some background in theoretical mathematics, more than they credit me with understanding, and I have been over these figures. It cannot possibly work. As the charts are constructed, the ship will definitely miss the Venus orbit and fall straightway into the sun. Of course you want to keep this highly confidential," Josephson said and began to work with knife and fork on a meat dish. "There's no point in making complications for them."

"If that's so," Evans said, "if that's really *so*, we've got to tell them. Right now."

"Not at all," said Jackson with a shrug and examined the bare walls of the empty commissary. As regulations provided, they always ate in a deserted room reconverted for their exclusive use. "They certainly won't listen to us and they'll call me hysterical. The best mathematicians and physicists in the world have worked on these charts for three years, you understand. You can hardly believe that they'd listen to me. No, it would come to nothing. All that they would do would be to bump me right out of the voyage and into an examination center, and they'd do it to you too and start all over again with the next on the list."

"But that's impossible," Evans said. "You just can't sit there so coldly and say something like that and do nothing."

"I didn't say I'd do nothing. I said that I wouldn't discuss it with them. The ship will definitely fail in orbit and fall into the sun. They have not taken into account the facts that Venus is far closer to the sun than any other body we've attempted and that the sun's gravity at certain delicate points will exceed that of Venus, even with the ship close in. The solar system is in continual disruption; there are waves of dislocation moving out from the sun at crucial times and at crucial points, and there is no way, as we settle in and move toward orbit, that we can avoid an interception. Sunspots, you know. These are the keys to the dislocation. The gravitational dislocations move out from the sunspots."

As he continued speaking, Jackson's face became flushed, his voice became higher and higher in pitch, and it occurred to Evans, looking at him, that the Captain might be demented and that the stress of training might have made him megalomaniacal. At the same time, as one of the prime conditions of his role, the training process had drilled into him the most unquestioning obedience of and reverence for the Captain. He therefore laid a steadying hand upon Josephson's and said, "Well, then, what do we do? What can we do?" noting that the Captain's hand was somewhat larger and rounder than his own and at the moment was infested by a peculiar kind of shakiness that scattered droplets of sweat on Evans' steadier member. "We've got to do something."

"We will," Jackson said, putting down his fork and looking at Evans straightforwardly, a slight twinkle in his calm gray eyes, a quick hand moving toward his hairline to adjust the service cap which he wore at all times in the commissary, "we will make the adjustments ourselves en route. It's very simple; it's a question of picking up the rhythm of the emanations as we approach Venus and then feeding them into the hand computer. We can do it easily once we apprehend the forces. We'll make the readjustments and bypass the computer block completely. No one will know. No one will ever know and we will orbit safely."

"But can we do that?"

"Of course we can do that," the Captain said. "I'm a fully trained mathematician; at least I'm sufficiently well trained to have detected the error originally. Trust me," he said, taking Evans' elbow gently between his hands and stroking it. "I'm the commander. Everything will be all right. I'm just telling you this so that you will be fully briefed and in a state of preparedness."

"But wouldn't it be easier," Evans asked, picking at his food, looking up uneasily at the ceiling to wonder for the first time if the commissary was monitored, "wouldn't it simply be easier to tell them what you've discovered? They could then make the corrections themselves, and surely the bank of computers would be far more effective than cruder calculations. They'd be glad to know—"

"No," Joseph Jackson said and removed his cap, twirled it on a finger, looked at the floor and then intently at Evans, "no, they wouldn't be glad to know. It wouldn't work. It couldn't possibly work. All that they would do would be to postpone the voyage and find another crew. They would think me mad. Do you think I'm mad, Evans?"

"Well, no—"

"I am not mad," Josephson said. "I am superbly qualified. On the other hand, the program is in very severe trouble. It has the Mars disaster behind it; it has the various failures of the moon, a whole tradition of failed planning and stupid maneuvering; and this Venus expedition was put together hastily and in the worst of circumstances. For political reasons and to save the program from complete dissolution. Don't you know that?"

"I've always suspected—"

"Suspect nothing! Apprehend! The program is riddled with disasters, supported by graft, and enacted through bureaucracy and stupidity. They misjudged the Venus orbit, didn't they? As I told you, this thing has been so poorly calculated that we would perish by incineration. Now, if they're so truly incompetent, Evans, that they would allow a misjudgment of this sort to be programmed into the flight, what do you think our chances would be in bringing it to their attention? No, we must take strong action. Independent, unswerving, highly individualized action. This program was originally conceived by highly individualized, courageous, idiosyncratic men; we must act within their tradition. Bureaucracy came after the fact. No, on the way to Venus we will take this data to the computer," Josephson said, "and we will resolve the problem ourselves. In fact, we will never tell them of the problem. That is the best way."

"I don't like it," Evans said, making a last desultory effort at his food and then putting it away; during the training program Evans had had little luck with his food in any event—for reasons which went far beyond simple fear—and now he could not even make a pretense of interest. "I think it would be better to bring it to the agencies'—"

"Agencies!" Jackson screamed and made a swipe with his hand, a gesture simultaneously so awkward and devastating that Evans pulled his chair back from the table, moved himself awkwardly over one of the arms of the chair, despite all of his training almost lost his balance enough to fall hopelessly to the floor, "enough of agencies! We have taken away the highly individualized, idiosyncratic effort and have put it in the hands of mindless, corrupted bureaucrats; bureaucrats who shield themselves through all their devices and have so subsumed the program within themselves that it is the individuals like ourselves who feel like the freaks. Put no trust in agencies, Evans; they occupy the least common denominator of human space. No," he said, leaning forward and throwing a palm against Evans' in a sudden horrid expansiveness, his eyes winking madly in the healthy, bland pan of his face, "no, this is between us. Just you and I, Evans; we will solve the problem. It will be just you and me in the capsule pelting toward Venus, the two of us to accomplish the orbit and the landing ourselves; their devices mean nothing, they exist only to limit our free will. We will conquer the computers ourselves.

"No," Josephson said, standing, still winking merrily, his fists in counterpoint clenching and unclenching rhythmically, panels of sweat glistening from his forehead, small burps and hisses coming from his mouth as he took a napkin to shield himself, as it were, from the onslaught of regurgitation, "no, this has nothing to do with them. It has only to do with us. What I've told you I've told you in great confidence and it is not to go beyond this table. But then if it did," he added, wiping his lips for the third time and then with a satisfied flourish putting the napkin away in his breast pocket, "if it did, it would only accomplish the cancellation of the voyage anyway, which is hardly what you would want, is it now? You want to land on Venus, don't you, Evans? You want to be a hero." And saying nothing else he strode magnificently from the cafeteria, his palms beating against hips, hips shrugging his fine legs, legs twinkling in anticipation of his feet, and his feet hitting the floor in a peculiar off-rhythm.

Evans stayed behind. Evans sat alone at the table and after a fashion and through great will and self-discipline, finished his lunch. This is something that Evans had learned early on in the program; it was best to take what they put before you because you never knew what the alternatives might be. Food was food, lunch was lunch, and the revelations of the Captain, small pellets of gloom, were absorbed within him with the same lack of discrimination, the same stolid insistence with which Evans ate: fruit cocktail supreme, roast prime ribs of beef au jus, mushrooms à la Luna, milk à la Holstein, and cured and curried ice cream from the deepest hydroponic farms of the old Syracuse complex, now moved to the dead Lake Michigan area, their synthetic cows bleating like real ones as the dead eyes, glowing like filaments, responded to the thud of the milking machine displacing the chemicals from them.

# 33

The Captain's name was Jack Josephson. No, it was Joseph Jackson. It was either Jack Josephson or Joe Jackson, but in either event it was no other and it is possible to make simple calculations from this interposition.

Piece by piece, it seems to be funneling into me. I will make an anagram of JOSEPHSON. It would be simplest to start in that way; the anagram could be the key to everything.

JOSEPHSON

SOJPHEON

PHONEJOS

JONES HOP

P O H JONES

NO JESPOH

ON JES HOP

My wife appears before me. Somehow she has managed to find her way into my room. This is not impossible; my wife follows me everywhere and there are no easy answers to this angle.

"You must live your life," she says, using an index finger to point out the cryptograms and through some delicacy of gesture, her contempt for all of them. "You must come to terms. You must understand that only you are inside your life and that there is no one else; that what you do you must stand by forever and it is only this one time around." She seems to be naked. She shows me her body in little flickers and shades: bounce of nipple, hint of snatch, whiff of thigh. "Here," she says, pointing into her cunt. "Here it is. Here is your reality." Her nipples are not erect. Her eyes are neutral and without feeling. "That is what you must discover."

"No," I say, "I don't believe that. There is something else, something beyond this," and reach to touch her, show her with cold fingers how little I feel for her, but she laughs and withdraws, her breasts bouncing in the dark, little cracks and chinks of the spectrum coming from her flesh as she moves away again.

"The mound of Venus," she says, "they call it the mound of Venus!" and laughs at me with sudden gaiety which we never had when we lived together and then disappears, leaving me with further conundrum while I shake my head in wonder at the devices that will persist, beyond their necessity, to move me.

PO JESHNO
SEJPO NOH
HONE JOPS
ONE J HOPS

# 34

I dream that I am talking to my dead uncle about the voyage, about all that has happened, and about what has happened to me since last we met. My uncle has been dead twenty years, seven months, and some days—which would seem to imply a certain amount of decomposition—but there he is, exactly as I knew him in life, a little while before the cancer which killed him came out of the gall bladder like a faulty apogee and slew him. He is smoking an archaic nicotine cigarette and sitting with familiar ease in his old lounge chair; although the dream is not clear for time and place, it appears that I am seeing him, as I occasionally used to, at the end of his day's work in the construction firm that he headed and now, his nap and Scotch ingested, he has become talkative and almost tolerant of me. "A good thing," he is saying. "Nevertheless, and despite all of that, a good thing. Man must conquer. Man must move onward. Venus is a wonderful goal."

Apparently the dream is *in medias res;* in any event, we seem to be deeply engrossed, as we always were during that adolescent series of discussions which in some obscure way I forgot when I entered the program. I have already told him all about the history of my involvement: the apprenticeship, the commission, the tests, the selection, the training program, and the actual events of the voyage itself, with their pitiful aftermath in this institution. I wish that the dream had picked up somewhat earlier in time so that I, as well as he, would then know what happened on the flight, but one cannot have everything; it is a pleasure to talk to my uncle after a lapse of so many years, and from the appearance of the glowing room, the half-filled Scotch glasses, the slow curls of deadly smoke from his cigarette holder, it appears that we are having a good time. "So even though it ended up that way you still think it justified," I say.

"Anything is justified," he says, "if it will lead man outward. Accomplishment, struggle, striving, the movement toward the goal. Man is the only one of God's creatures that can conceive of a goal in abstract terms, that can sacrifice his life toward that attainment. Venus. Wonderful! The moon. Wonderful! When I died, you know, they were just starting the suborbital flights and no one believed. But I had faith even then. Of course, I was too busy to take much of an interest, but I knew. I knew it would come to this."

"Mars," I say. "You haven't mentioned Mars."

"Mars was unfortunate," my uncle says, "but this is the price you must pay for achievement. Struggle, suffering, loss, pain. Only the game fish can swim upstream, you know." He is racked by a hopeless siege of coughing which drives his head helplessly further and further toward the floor; at last his forehead is stopped by his knees and he lies against them for a moment, then slowly eases himself to a sitting position, stabbing out the cigarette in short, trembling bursts. "Fucking cigarettes," he says. "They were what did it to me, you know. I had no luck. If I had been born twenty years later or if the cancer had just held out a little while, they would have switched to the nicotineless brands and I would have been able to hear the whole thing myself instead of getting it secondhand from a distant relative. Tell me more, son," he says, "tell me what Venus is like. I'm very interested in Venus; in any new frontier, any new pole of human accomplishment. After all, that's what I'm in the construction business for, not just for the money but to expand, to create new things. What is it like? Beautiful, I betcha. It's the nearest planet to the sun, isn't it?"

"No," I say, "it's the second. Earth is the third. We flew from the third to the second. But I can't tell you about Venus because we never got there. It has heavy cover formed by gases and vapors and no one knows what's on the surface. We still don't know. Now we'll never know."

"Why not? So you failed, what does that mean? There will be a second flight and a third and a fifth. Eventually you'll conquer Venus. That's in the cards. We got Mexico, didn't we? California? The South Pole? Once we decide to do something, nothing can stop us. That's mankind. That's all of us," my uncle says and stands, swaying slightly, his dressing gown floating in the strange breeze which seems to be in these spaces, momentarily confused as he looks beyond his easy chair and my own straightback, puzzled that there is nothing in the distance but a clear, gray mist. "Well," he says, "this has been very interesting, but I don't have much more time. I have things to do, appointments to keep. It's still very interesting and nothing changes, you know. You take care of yourself, Harry, will you?"

"You don't understand," I say. "You haven't even let me finish. I want to know what to do. I've got to get some advice. I've come to ask you for help."

"I have no advice."

"You were the only man I ever knew who talked the way you did. You believed that there were rational solutions to rational problems and that it was only a matter of making the engineering work. You had faith, a belief, a certain conviction in human destiny . . ." and then I cannot go on; I seem to be crying. Choking sobs well from me; I conceal them with a forearm and force myself to continue. "You can't just leave," I say, "you have to give me some answers. What do I do? What do we do next? What's going to happen to us?"

"The same things that will always happen. We'll voyage on and on."

"And me? What about me?"

"I'm afraid that you'll have to work out for yourself," my uncle says vaguely. "I can't get involved in particulars, you know; generalizations were always my specialty. Well," he says, standing awkwardly—a certain unease in his gait and unsteadiness in his legs—and weaving his way out of my line of sight, "this has been truly interesting and I'm delighted to know that you've done so well, Harry. Keep up the good work and everything will be resolved in the long run." He looks stricken, a slow look of dismay passing from eyes to forehead and then bouncing down to his cheekbones; he puts a fingernail against his mouth in puzzlement. "I know I forgot something," he says. "Oh, yes; oh, yes, that's it. Money. Do you need any money, Harry? You would always hint around for money after our discussions. If you need any—"

"No," I say. "My needs are provided for here."

"I was just going to say that if you needed any there's nothing I can do for you because my sources of income seem to have been taken away. So you'll have to work that out for yourself, son. Anyway, the important thing is that we had a good talk, didn't we? And I straightened you out."

"But you haven't answered anything," I say. "You've left me the same as before. I still don't know why—"

"You've got to stop this, Harry," my uncle says and lays a ghostly, not unpleasant hand upon my shoulder, sending small waves of irradiation palpitating down the line of the arm, "and not ask so many questions. I never had any patience with your questions, Harry: to tell you the truth, I just made up the answers that seemed to fit, but I am not a reflective man. Action, accomplishment—that's all that matters, of course, over the age of twenty-one," my uncle says and quickly leaves the line of sight; I am standing in pools of grayness as his easy chair contracts into a small ball and is yanked out of the area, the lights go down, I seem to have no clothing on; I am very embarrassed.

"Answers," I say, "I want the easy answers; you always had them, you can't run out on me now, you can't do this to me; you've got to come to the point," and so on and so forth, but my uncle is out of the picture, my voice sounds petulant and juvenile in my ears and the scene mercifully blanks out totally; I am back in my bed, crawling out of the dream in small pieces, sweating and fussing, muttering to myself, or perhaps I am only clambering back into a dream, coming into my room in small sections, but in any event it is very complex and uncontrollable and I can make nothing of it, so after a time I get up from the bed and sit in the chair for a time, contemplating.

At least my wife is not loose in the halls tonight. No one is scrabbling with fingers at my door. I am glad that they have stopped that nonsense. I am entitled to the integrity of this room, not that any of it has come to resolution.

I remember how my uncle looked the last time I saw him and can only admire the restorative benefits of death; he looks better than he had in many years and seems very positive and forward-thinking, not to say pleased with how well his philosophy stands up in the technological age.

# 35

"We are going to Venus," I say to the Captain, "because it is populated and it is planned that we will sign a treaty of everlasting peace and friendship with the Venusians, thereby inaugurating several generations of peace and progress. Hidden in the hold are the documents, all signed and notarized on our end. You have been keeping this from me until the landing as a pleasant surprise. You are quite aware of the presence of Venusians on the planet and in due course are authorized to make a deal."

"No," the Captain says and chuckles. His eyes are quite wild. He seems progressively abstracted. "That is not the way it worked out at all. Guess again, Evans. Keep them coming. You must make a more serious effort to solve the problem; this voyage is not limitless, and besides, you should show some will and application, discipline and meaning." He burps, shifts abruptly on the chair, makes a discommoding kick, and lands on the floor. "Hurry," he says, ignoring his collapse. "Hurry; get to the point. You've got to overreach yourself, Evans; get to the point now or you'll never have a chance to ask me about my sex life. Don't you want to know about my sex life?" he says with a leer. "There are things you never dreamed possible that I could tell you, and frankly, I'm aching to take you into my confidence because all of this interplanetary space, to say nothing of the conversations with the Venusians, is making me extremely horny, but fair's fair and we must stick with the rules of the game. What benefits for any of us could there be if we don't accept our own strictures, have the integrity of our own decisions? No, Evans, you must do better," he says and reseats himself upon the chair with a thud, placing his elbows on his knees and resting his chin on his hands, a peculiar and intense gleam coming from his damaged eyes. "Come on," he says, "I'll give you a hint. It has something to do with our personal lives. There is a direct *personal* reason why the two of us are on this ship. Look at it from that aspect: private motives, private goals. Does that help? Does that help?" the Captain asks and slides from the chair in a dead faint; I must resuscitate him with glasses of water and some gestures of respiration until at last he puffs and turns over and the game, always the game, resumes.

# 36

Following through on an old political pledge made by a leader of the discredited administration, men embarked for Mars in 1976. A standard crew of three were involved on the flight. Embarkation was from moon orbit, transfer to the larger ship being made there because of the cheaper costs of final assembly and fuel allowing escape velocity from that satellite. The voyage was scheduled to last six weeks: two weeks toward Mars, two weeks back, and the remainder for actual exploration and mapping of the red planet. According to official statement the three men composing the crew were the most highly qualified team in the history of the project, although only one of them had actually participated in the earlier abandoned moon program. The other two were scientists: a physicist and a biologist, given heavy physical training, to turn the voyage into one of exploration and achievement. The program was responding to popular objections from the media that the moon program had been poorly rationalized, formulated with no clear outcome, and was largely a public relations ploy without true scientific substance or value.

Mars is the fourth planet from the sun in this solar system. It is known as the red planet because early observations detected it as being surrounded by a reddish glow. Whether this was spectral distortion from the atmosphere or whether the sands and grounds of the planet itself were actually tinted red was one of the numerous and interesting questions which the expedition was to answer. Some of the other questions which the expedition was to answer were among the following:

1)  Is there intelligent life on Mars?
2)  Is there any life on Mars?
3)  Are the famous Martian canals geological formations which coincidentally obey laws of geometric relation and appear to run in straight lines, or are they the remnants of a powerful and intelligent race, now extinct, which constructed them as a way of conveying water across their parched and stricken planet?
4)  Are the canals phenomena created by a race which is *not* extinct and would that race yield an explanation of their function?
5)  Deimos and Phobos, two satellites of the fourth planet, are immeasurably smaller in proportion to their parent body than any other moons in the solar system. Their peculiar and opposed orbits are also unique, as well as certain indications through spectral study that they may be metallic in construction. Are they, therefore, artificial satellites, constructed by an intelligent race who placed them in their orbits for experimental or technological purposes?
6)  Can Mars yield anything worthwhile in either experimental knowledge or produce to mankind?
7)  In light of the expensive and essential failure of the Apollo project, can a carefully underpublicized and ostensibly scientific investigation of the planet Mars redeem for the discredited space project, and for the uneasy administration which oversees it, enough credit to justify the expense in terms of time and materials?

On May 4, 1976, the *Kennedy II*, with its small and well-trained crew, embarked on its flight to solve these as well as some other essential mysteries.

# 37

"One human being is nothing," Forrest must have said to me, "no matter the investment, no matter the relationship, no matter the circumstances; in the long run, we must essentially take a cheap view of human life if we are to get anywhere. This was the mistake of the original planners of the program: they valued human life too highly because of the publicity in which these projects took place, and resultantly, progress was slowed by years, perhaps by decades. We could have had a man on the moon in 1958 or maybe 1953 if the value of life had not been misproportioned to that of research. But that will end. That is ending. We are no longer going to make these mistakes.

"We are, in short," he must have said, leaning closer to me, looking more menacing as he did this, increasing my dislocation and sense of loss, "going to find out what happened, and if we can elicit this information only through painful means, then this is the way in which it will have to be. We do not have the time, Evans, do not have the respect for mysteries, which we might have tolerated at one time: we will approach this in simple, practical ways and we will find what we must. That is your mistake, Evans. You misjudged us. You did not think that we were serious about this, and your training might have given you a disproportionate self-evaluation, but you are in for an unpleasant shock.

"No one man is that important, Evans. You mean nothing to us. You are an informational tool; that is all the two of you ever were, and we are going to get the information in any way we can. Voluntarily or involuntarily. I realize that there is a cost invoked here and it may cost you some pain, but that is the way it must be. I will not apologize.

"Now, Evans, will you be reasonable or must we take measures?" I think he asked and I said nothing; how could I say anything, I lay in ice, sheets of fire surrounding me, the hard, cold eyes of attendants I could not touch tossing sphincters of pain, and I tried to say something but could not. "All right," I think he said then, "that is what I suspected. So be it then, so be it; let the process begin," and I was taken out of there, saw nothing until much later.

Surely he must have said this to me. It is the only explanation. If he did not say this to me, then all of this is going on outside of my mind and for all I know I might still be in the ship: locked into the latest and greatest of the Venusian Disturbances, scaled aliens merrily inserting their probes while I lie narcotized and anguished beneath machinery, pouring my secrets into their circuitry, which can only transmit all of this to small jolts and bright flashes on the ribbons which record.

# 38

"Why not a child?" Evans said to his wife in the aftermath of intercourse, seeing her lie flushed and open under him, an illusion of accessibility which she always had at those times before everything became irretrievably ugly. "I see nothing wrong with it."

"No," she said, "no, under no circumstances," and pivoted under him, swinging neatly to her side of the bed, unbalancing an arm and causing him to topple, abruptly, on his haunches. "I won't have it."

"We will someday, you know."

"No, we won't. Not if I have anything to say about it. Never, never."

"We have to think of the future. This isn't going to last forever, you know."

"You want it to," she said to the helpless and stammering Evans. "You have no sense of time at all. You think that it's going to last."

"No, I don't."

"Yes, you do and besides I don't want to talk now because that only means fighting and I'm tired. I want to go to sleep."

"Hey," the discombobulated Evans said, running a forefinger across the slickness of her cheek, "hey, remember something. I'm trying to take a flight. I might wind up on a ship to Venus or somewhere. It isn't impossible. The odds are against it, but they're against anyone. Doesn't that mean anything to you?"

"This program is your life."

"But it's your life too."

"Not if I can help it, and I really want to go to sleep; I can't stand these discussions any more."

"Think of me," Evans, reaching for his clothing, said, inserting a leg into his underpants. "Think of me heading out there, thirty-five million miles to Venus. Don't you think I'd want to know that there's something of me left here? A child, a successor? It isn't easy for me, you know."

"Great. So get out of the program."

"I will. I will. But not just now. I have to stay in now; you know the conditions."

"Get out of the program and we'll talk about many things."

"You promised," he said, running a hand across the back of her neck, feeling the smooth, mindless rise of blood under his palm. "You said that if I really wanted to stay you wouldn't object. So I really wanted to stay."

"So I haven't stopped you. Stay. See if I stop you. Don't you realize that I don't have that much feeling about this any more? I just don't care, but you've got to stop talking with me this way. I gave you sex, didn't I? I've never held out on you sexually and you can make damned sure that I'm not going to have a child to top that off. I kept every part of the bargain. Now if you're not going to sleep, I am," she said and dead-naked shut off the light on her side of the bed and managed to at least simulate the rhythms of somnolence.

Evans, stricken, bemused, humbled, helpless, lay there for a time, picking specks of dirt from the sheet with his fingernail and looking at the insects dazzling themselves to death on the bulb above. The light burned his eyes and eventually he closed them, but even so shrouded, he still saw the bulb, hanging like a pudenda just behind his vision, insects battering and battering their way against it; heat rising and arching, shimmering like death to his eyes while his wife lay the night and slept a sleep with moans. He forgets how the issue of a child came out. He forgets how it was resolved. He is not sure whether they ended by having a child or not but he is pretty sure, as much as he can recollect things, that they did not. He hopes not.

# 39

On their first day together in the simulator the Captain, Joseph Jackson, turned to Evans and against the whining and bucking of the machinery, said, "For all we know, we could be on our way to Venus now. Perhaps we aren't in a laboratory at all. Doesn't that frighten you?"

Evans shook his head, not willing to speak, trying to hold his teeth against the retching which seemed at any moment calculated to send his insides into the bucket thoughtfully provided. The simulator was bearing down with jolts of eighteen gravities in short bursts to prepare them for the actual shock of acceleration and orbital maneuver, and Evans found himself in and out of consciousness all the time: spacing out the faints with dry heaves and blinding gurgles of pain, waiting for the next jolt. He had never been in the simulator with the Captain before nor had he been under such heavy pressure. But flight time was approaching and he understood that they wanted to move closer to actual conditions and into a dual-occupancy situation. "Nothing frightens me," Evans said, at that time being distracted by terror and in addition being locked deep into what he would come to think of afterwards as his Gray Period. "There's nothing that they can do to me that I don't know . . ." and then the next jolt hit him like a pint of gin and he found himself gasping, holding on for balance against the slick walls, his shoulders pinned to the floor, his detumescent—in fact, vanishing—phallus sending its own peculiar messages of travail to him. "Well, maybe not," Evans said.

"You see," Jackson said with something approaching imperturbability, although if Evans had cared to look, he might have seen the distinct madness in his eyes, "we have absolutely no control over our lives. None whatsoever; they have taken that away from us. We exist only for their pleasure." He rubbed his hands against one another with immense casualness, studied his palms. He could be sitting as dummy at a bridge table, Evans thought, considering the intracacies of a hand. "The control they give us is only an illusion," the Captain said and then with an absent distinctness retched, allowed dry heaves to overtake him as once again they went into a spin. "But I know the secret," he said when they returned to normal pressure, "I still have something over them."

"What could that be?" Evans said with mild, polite curiosity, wondering if he would live to get out of the chamber. "What do you have over them?"

"Oh, not now," Jackson said with a cackle and gave Evans a light tap on the shoulder as once again the gravities increased. There was very little time for conversation in the chamber. "I couldn't possibly tell you now; they might be monitoring everything in here, our reactions and so on. No, I will tell you that later. Later, Evans, on the way to Venus," said Joseph Jackson and the chamber spun, the walls contracted, Evans fainted and the preparations thus continued, only the curiously fixated stare of the unfainting Captain's eyes remaining with the highly distorted Evans as he passed into unconsciousness.

# 40

In the morning my wife comes to see me. She addresses me through a small opening in a special cubicle while two attendants, arms folded, stand behind her and favor me with winks and grimaces. A sensual leer now and then seems to pass over the face of the older guard, some apprehension of what my wife and I have been through together. On the other hand, there seems to be little interest in sexuality in this institute and I may be imagining all of this. "This is the last time," she says, gathering her coat around her and favoring the wall over my right shoulder with a dazzling, abstract stare. "I'm not coming back here again. I just wanted to tell you that this was the last time."

"Fine," I say, exchanging winks with the older guard and looking down at my pants leg, which seems to be clotted with semen. Nocturnal or daily emissions seem almost impossible under these circumstances; nevertheless, the stiffness, the resilience of the fabric is unmistakable. I wonder what I have been up to. "If that's necessary."

"I'm leaving here. I'm going a long, long way and I won't be coming back. The papers will go through automatically. Do you hear what I'm saying, Harry?"

"Not if you look over at the wall."

"I'm coming to tell you because I think you ought to know. But I have nothing else to say."

She is really an attractive woman, I finally decide (I have been in doubt about my wife's objective appearance for many years): the bluntness of her features, the hard arch of her breast, calculate effects where a hint of delicacy might lose them, and her fingers are knifed to the bone with small scratches and nervous little excisions of fingernails; then again, the things that she did to her hands always excited me—I remember now—when she placed them on me. "Fine," I say to this attractive woman whom I have decided I do not want to hurt, "you're going to go far away and the papers will come through later, so there's nothing for me to do. They gave you permission. Permission to go away." I exchange a meaningful look with the older guard and gather my features together so that he will understand that I have fucked this woman with whom I am talking; granting this confirmation can only make his fantasies more satisfying. The younger guard, who has until now ignored the relationship which has been established, shakes his head and uses a club to make small scratches against the wall behind him, throwing the club absently over his shoulder in a backhanded way. I try with various small encouraging looks and indications to include him in the situation, but he seems to want none of it. "So you're going," I continue, "and that's what you came to tell me."

"Yes," she says. She leans toward me, places her hands against the wall underneath the open space, furls her finger. "I just wanted to tell you that in a way I felt very guilty for a long time, but now I don't feel any guilt at all. It isn't my fault, it isn't my fault, and now I can leave. I'm through feeling involved, Harry."

"Certainly," I say. "I understand perfectly. You're through

being involved and there's no reason for you to feel guilty, so now you've decided to go away. Whatever has happened to me came out of individual factors or maybe what happened during the flight, so you aren't implicated. Not at all. Implicated." I lean against her, forehead to forehead, admire the cool panels of her skin, the hint of her lips retreating from me. "So that's what you came to tell me and you told me, so now you can go."

"That's the way it always was. You don't listen."

"I listen to everything," I say. "Don't I listen?" I ask the old guard. He stares blankly. "I asked you, don't I listen to everything that goes on here? Am I not attentive?"

"I guess you're attentive," he says. "I don't know anything about it."

"Don't talk to him," the other guard says. "We're not supposed to talk to him, remember? Shut up or I'll report you."

"He can talk to me if he wants to. He has the same civil-service rights and privileges that you do. Anyway, he just wants to get on my good side. He just wants to fuck my wife."

"That's all," she says, standing. "That's the end."

"He wants to fuck my wife; well, why not? What's so unhealthy about that? What have I said that's wrong? Everybody wants to fuck an astronaut's wife; it's a little piece of America right there and ready to be realized. It would be abnormal not to want to fuck you. Everybody does, you know. In fact," I say, rising with her, "in fact, everybody has."

Her hand is quick; I can feel the skidding contact made and broken, but the young guard is even faster; he has traversed the space between them almost as quickly as her hand has made the smaller distance to my face and now he seizes her by the wrist, looks at her with a curious apathy, and says, "Don't touch him. Don't you ever do that again. You're not supposed to touch him; no one is."

"That's right," I say. "I'm aseptic."

"Let me," she says, struggling, "let me, let me—" and it takes both guards, the older one surprisingly more graceful and poised than the younger, to back her into the opposite wall; she stands there for a while heaving, her handbag trembling against her shoulder, and I can see, looking with my keen and usual intentness, all of the emotions scurrying within her toward their separate and familiar cubicles. Doors slam all up and down my wife's body; lights are extinguished. She pants, she groans. Her nostrils flare. "That it had to end this way," she says, "that's the only regret. That it had to end this way." She tries to shrug off the guards' embrace, make her exit that way, but the guards, stolid men for all of their diverse fantasies, have no understanding of drama and timing and will not release her. Like a fish she struggles against their hands, awkward with surprise, but then she sees that they will not release her and tumbles within herself again. "Oh, for God's sake," she says, raising a forearm in a constricted way to brush hair from her eyes, "I'm not going to hit again. I just want to *leave* him."

"We have to escort you out, lady," the older guard says, running an unprofessional hand across her wrist and then up to her shoulder blade. "Visitors must be escorted. Particularly when you did what you did. I have to tell them that, you know."

"So tell them."

"Listen," I say, poking my head and shoulders out of the open space so that I can gesture with fluid ease, take over the situation, so to speak, control it by letting my own thoughts be known, "leave her alone. It's perfectly all right; you don't have to report what she did. It didn't hurt me and anyway it was a family quarrel. Actually, she's a very limited person and she can only control scenes as she stages them. She has very little imagination. Pity is called for. You should pity this woman."

"No," the younger guard says, shaking his head, "you stay out of it. You're not allowed to talk. Get back inside there before I make you."

"There's no need to threaten. What are my options? Considering what she's had to work with for most of her life, I think that she's doing very well. Don't you think you're doing well?" I ask her, meaning to add her name, but I have forgotten her name and still cannot recollect it . . . and this onslaught of the old vagueness at exactly the moment in which I am trying to master a situation quite overcomes me, and shamed, I withdraw myself back into the cubicle and sit on the facing chair. "I'm sorry," I say, feeling a tearing sob, self-sentimentalization surely, working its way out of me. "I'm sorry, I'm sorry."

"Bad," the younger guard says, "it's very bad," and I do not know if he is referring to my situation or the overall civil-service prospect as he sees it; in any event, he says no more and the two of them, muttering to one another, take my wife away. She passes out of the pan of my vision and I hear a door switch open and shut. Just as she passes through the door I remember her name and bolt to my feet. "Helen!" I say. "Helen, you can't do this to me! you've got to stay here; someone's got to stay to see what they've done to me!" But she is gone and all that I manage to do is to give myself a stinging clout on the head—wetness, pain, disorientation—and I fall to my knees in surprise and two other attendants (they always come in twos) are there to support me and there I am in their arms, being carried to my room, murmuring *Helen, Helen, Helen* but where is she now or for that matter Claude Forrest so that they can admire this latest and truly greatest signature of my promise? *Helen, you bitch, you knew everything first,* I seem to be saying obscurely, but a spaceman's head, like a crucifix, is impermeable and all of this carelessness will accomplish nothing. It has accomplished nothing so far; surely these conditions will continue.

"Damn you, Helen," I say and with cunning and care the attendants replace me in my little room and lock the door behind, so that if I only will, I am free for all of the afternoon to curse her, but I do not, I do not curse her; I look over in the corner instead, on my table, and urging will and discipline upon myself, continue the bridge problem. There is no excuse for these emotional outbreaks. There is no excuse for these emotional outbreaks.

# 41

"I'm really sorry," West says to him, regret in his tone, regret bringing his stout features to an unnatural flush, "I'm really sorry that I had to take that trick, Evans, but you know the contract was a cold set if I led the spades and I couldn't let you talk me out of it. You don't control the world, Evans: the world doesn't owe you a living, you've got to understand that other people have options too.

"You see," West adds, in full explicative thrust, his amiable hands playing with the deck of cards as he does so, showing an ace, hiding a king, his twinkling eyes moving between walls and score sheet, "you've had the wrong idea about this from the first; you've looked at the hand from the wrong way out. Just because you're South doesn't mean that things revolve around you, you know: this could be a demonstration of faulty dummy play or then again how an ingenious set was devised. You must be tolerant: there are four players at the table and each of them, no less than you, is a human being, sunk into his own passions and vices, viewing himself as a *persona;* all along you've approached the problem without seeing the human element and that's your difficulty.

"But I do feel guilty that I cashed that trick, Evans," West concedes, shaking his head and now laying out the cards for the next deal, "you have a way of making me feel *culpable* somehow, so I do want to apologize, and apologize as well for that violent business afterwards. Maybe we can work it out so you'll win the next hand. Would that be all right? Would that be all right with you, huh?" West says and winks at Evans, favors him with a winning smile, begins with élan to deal out the cards, but Evans has not been able to take any of this in the spirit intended: no less than before, he is overcome by the spirit of West's treachery, the greed and insistence which would force this fat, insignificant defense man into taking an unnecessary trick and destroying Evans' solution; and so Evans—renewed by his conversation with his wife, his struggles with the attendant, his ever-increasing memories of what has happened to him—renewed by all of this, Evans throws himself straight at West's pasty throat; groaning, he seizes the enemy's flesh and seeks to strangulate, but at that moment the door is flung open and Bridge Experts come in: here they come in a slow, solemn procession, five or six beady-eyed men wearing double-breasted suits and carrying cigarettes in long holders. "Stop that now!" they cry. "We will have none of this; it is against the rules of the Stayman Convention, and in any event, the finest clubs would not tolerate your behavior. You must always bid an automatic peremptory no-trump in order for your partner to show his minors; you must lead through the strength of your opponents; you must maintain decorum in this great game," and the Bridge Experts use their scrawny but amazingly efficient hands and arms to tear Evans from West's throat and toss him trembling into a corner. "Sons of bitches," Evans cries without conviction, "it isn't fair; you can't do this to me," his voice curiously a whine, not an accusation, and as West pats his lapels, rearranges his clothing, breathes his thanks to the experts for their help, the experts consult among one another and then very efficiently proceed to gather around the table and deal out a hand for themselves as West kibitzes and Evans lies murmuring in a corner. "One no-trump," the first expert says, "pass," "pass," "double" and "pass," "pass" and "redouble," "pass," "pass," "pass," and with consummate and exquisite haste the hand is played out, one no-trump redoubled making two, fifty points under the line, and then they stand, shake hands, and withdraw. "To Venus," one of them says. "To Venus!" they all say and they are gone except for West, who, puffing unpleasantly, sits awaiting Evans' pleasure at the empty table, making small doodles on the score sheet. "I don't think that these problems are working out the way they should," Evans says, and when West nods sadly, moistly, banishes him from the room and resolves to put that one part, if nothing else, of his life permanently from him.

# 42

During the Fourth Great Venusian Disturbance, Evans' mind is completely overtaken, and he is advised by the aliens that he will be taken on a guided tour of Venus. "Just be calm, don't fight us," the voices in his head advise him, "and remember that you're still in your craft; this is merely a kind of suggestive process we're using. We're by no means sufficiently developed to transport you physically." Then as he lies there paralyzed, his eyes closed (or perhaps they are open; he loses, practically speaking, all control over his consciousness), he is taken through Venus; he plunges beneath the cloud cover and there sees wondrous cities, great examples of architecture, fertile and lush fields on which Venusians, who look no less humanoid than men, toil happily. "The farms feed the cities, the cities sustain the farms, and united we prosper," his tour guides tell him and then he sees color pictures of industry and progress: enormous machinery and vehicles moving through the landscape. "We are a sedentary race, a mild and peace-loving race, dedicated not to exploration but to the preservation of our own; otherwise, we would have approached your planet hundreds of years ago and wiped you out," they explain to him as he sees close-up pictures of happy Venusians, presumably of opposite sexes, nuzzling one another while the machinery throws fire into the sky. "All that we desire is to live out our cycle, the days of our race, in peace and harmony. Those gases which you see are merely protective cover; we hoped that you would decide the planet was uninhabitable," they admit somewhat coyly, and then Evans sees pictures of dedicated Venusian scientists working in laboratories containing huge vats from the tops of which bubble gases that look very much like those astronomically noted. "However, we did not reckon with your persistence." Evans now sees flash-cuts and strobe-lit impressions of Venusian politicians and scientists meeting in huge panels, conferring solemnly with one another, and then more machinery, subtler this time and housed in banks which look like coffins. "So we settled on these defensive devices that would enable us to contact you and dispose of your craft if we must," the guide tells him, and then the picture blanks out, his mind becomes utterly dead and soft and then after a pause, Evans supposes, to change the reels of the projection, Evans sees a close-up of his own face. Sweating, demented, on the edge of consciousness, his face collides with disturbances in the air, seems to collapse, goes into utter repose and sleep. Evans understands that he is being shown his own appearance during the takeoff of the ship, but this does not enable him to bear it any more easily; he finds his own aspect horrifying and tries to close off the pictures . . . but the Venusians, cackling to one another when they see that they have had an effect upon him, will not stop and now Evans sees other pictures of himself: Evans defecating in the capsule, Evans eating, Evans in discourse with the Captain, Evans using the communicator to deliver a position, Evans subtly reaching toward his private parts during a sleep period and then masturbating himself ferociously. "Stop it, stop it!" Evans shrieks, quite unable to bear this, but the aliens are remorseless: they show him more clips, Evans in sleep, his face crinkling as the map of several nightmares which pass over him, Evans awakening to another day in the capsule, his eyes filling with the horror of recollection until he can pad them over, Evans putting huge wads of processed food into his mouth while looking crazily at the Captain, who seems to be in a still life of regurgitation. "Enough!" he shouts, "enough of this!" and only then do the aliens relent, the pictures go off, his mind becomes jelly again, and then quite gradually firms while behind his consciousness he has an impression of conference and reconnoitering; then his mind becomes firm and he finds that he is staring at the ceiling, seeing the humble inside of his own ship again and listening to the voices of the disturbance without visual aid. Somewhere off in the corner the Captain is jumping and thrashing; perhaps he is now seeing reels. "So you see," the voices say, "this is the position we've had to take. We have our own interests to consider, as well you know. We have our own planet, our own lives, to protect. So we must ask you to turn this craft around instantly or be destroyed."

"But it's nonsense!" Evans says. "Don't you understand; it's got to be hallucinatory. Venus is uninhabited; there's no such thing as intelligent life on Venus, and if there were, it would never take the forms you've shown me. This is all inside my own head, the whole thing has been self-created. It's the strain of space. The same thing must have happened on the way to Mars. I'm imagining all of this."

"I'm afraid you're not. Really, we're quite sympathetic to your point of view, but you imagine nothing. This is exactly the way it is. We can't account for the gaps in your own knowledge, the flaws of your own researchers."

"Neurasthenia," Evans says, beginning to get an understanding of the situation. "Neurasthenic hallucinations and withdrawal. We were warned about this. It's self-created, I knew it was. None of this is happening."

"It really is happening, Evans. We're quite serious and we're going to destroy your ship if you don't turn around. Either that or we'll destroy one of you and send the other back to pass the word we must not be bothered again. We haven't quite settled on which one it will be. Probably we'll just wipe you out. On the other hand, the psychology of the other way is somewhat sounder. It doesn't matter."

"No," Evans says, struggling on the bunk, forcing himself into a sitting position, "none of this. Not any more. Will, discipline, training, physical control. I will get hold of myself and I will deny all of this," and with a savage thrust of his mind succeeds in dispersing, at least temporarily, all of the elements of the disturbance; all of it flows away from him like water, and shaky and trembling he stands, his sense of triumph almost immediately deflected by shrill whines and shrieks which come from the Captain, thrashing on his bunk, his eyes closed, his hands clasped, his thighs rotating, his genitals bulging; the Captain's eyes then flinging themselves open to bulge as well, all of him open and distended, and watching the Captain, Evans becomes suddenly aware of exactly what pictures the aliens must be showing in the Captain's mind, for the Captain is indisputably coming . . . and Evans, who has never seen another man come before, finds this display so shocking and interesting that he kneels tailor-fashion, his chin cupped in his hand, to examine it more closely and his interest is so piqued, his involvement is so total, that he wonders if he does not, perhaps just a little bit, trust the aliens after all and accept the credibility of their mission.

# 43

It is time to tell all; I can no longer hold back. Past dissembling, past all maneuver, I take a clean sheet of paper, draw it to me, and without pretension or delay, commence to write. It is quiet in these rooms; no hint, for the moment, of observation: I can tell them everything and it will be as if I were merely talking to myself.

*Gentlemen,* I write, gentlemen, the true story of the 1981

Venus expedition may now be told. On our way there we were intercepted by Venusians (Venetians?), who took over our minds and showed us pictures in them. I saw travelogues of their planet but believe that the Captain saw something more overtly sexual. The Venusians warned us that if we did not immediately turn the mission around they would kill one of us and send the other back to give warning. They did not believe that we were incapable of manual override on the computers and therefore brutally slaughtered the Captain as an example case. I was so overwhelmed by the horror of this deed that I literally went into shock—a cataleptic state with neurasthenic overtones intimating complete schizoid breakdown—and was unable until this moment to communicate the sense of what happened. Instead I retreated to disassociation reflex, blunted affect, and the characteristic small obsessions of the schizoid: puzzles, games, and false, obsessive recollections. Even the efforts of my wife to reach me were unsuccessful. However, thanks to the devoted efforts of the institutional staff and particularly due to the professional dedication and concern of the senior psychiatrist on duty, Claude Forrest, I was slowly brought back into relation with reality and tonight, on this night, the very pieces fell together. I am therefore disclosing to you the total and ironic truth of what happened on the Venus flight; I am able at last to bear up under this revelation and hope, of course, that you will be as well.

It is a humbling thing, gentlemen, a humbling thing! to realize that there is at least one other intelligent race in our own small solar unit and that this race is capable of treating us so cruelly and egregiously. It was xenophobic pride along with guilt, I believe, that kept me from accepting this until now: I too did not want to believe in Venusians but instead was seeking some naturalistic outlet, some credible and limited explanation . . . but this was not to be. I hope that this news finds you well and now that I have at last yielded the full and final explanation of the Venus disaster, you will close down these walls and allow me to come out from between them as a free man. I would like to walk in the sun with my wife. I would like to pump her thighs and feel the sticky mingled fluids of release. I would like to attend a large reception in one of our major cities, one in which I will be granted a medal of honor and allowed to take the flag. I would appreciate a ticker-tape parade down the canals of old Broadway, just the dignitaries and me sitting hoisted over the rear parapet of the car, floating in storms or streams of sound, the faint intimation of an assassin's bullet prodding from the back of consciousness to keep me from thinking too much of myself.

I would like to retire from the program and join one of the ministries or become a cabinet functionary. I would like to advise the President on this matter or that and have photographs of us published: two serious, dedicated faces, convoluted with discussion, smirking at the camera. I would like to own a 1975 Cadillac with automatic sentinel and turbine release, a wish which for its own reasons the program never granted me. I would eventually like to become attached to one of the universities as a consultant. I would like to live out the spaces of my life in amusement parks, narcotics parlors, and board rooms. I do not think that this is unreasonable. I think that I have a perfect right to these ambitions. I wish to forget about Venusians, the program, Venus, the Captain, test flights, the program, the compression chamber, cryptograms, the program, and many other things. *Yours as ever faithfully,* and signing my name in the requisite way I shove this paper, like all the others, underneath the door of my room and wait for it to be taken, wait for the door to be pulled open, wait for the reaction which will free me.

# 44

Jackson. His name was Joseph Jackson. There are several anagrams of Jackson, although of course there are more anagrams of Josephson because the latter is the longer name. However, one must do with what one has and I distinctly remember that his name was Joseph Jackson—not Jack Josephson, as I once believed—as I circle nearer and nearer the truth.

JACKSON

SON JACK

SO JANCK

KNOS JAC

C K JANOS

K C JONAS

CANS JOCK

In the morning, and not before, Evans is aroused from his pained sleep and taken down the corridor and through an aperture, then taken into the office of Claude Forrest. Forrest, holding Evans' recent communication in his hand (Evans can recognize his own handwriting, the tinted paper on which he has been doing his correspondence, the shaky creases into which he had folded the paper before sliding it under the door), nods at Evans and motions for him to sit. Evans does so, fixing Forrest with an intense and tightening stare, his fine eyebrows crinkling, forehead pursing, intelligence flooding him as if coming from a suddenly opened tap, resolved now to show Forrest that he can be the man-he-always-was despite his recent adventures. "I read this," Forrest says, motioning toward the paper and then dropping it on his desk. "This is very interesting."

"Thank you," Evans says. Although he tries not to be moved, he feels a small gulp of pride moving within him. He has always wanted the admiration of Claude Forrest (he can admit that now), particularly for his writing style, which Evans considers unusual and highly literate, especially for an astronaut. "Thank you very much."

"Do you stand by this? Is this what you really want us to believe?"

Shakily, Evans nods. "Yes," he says, "that is as I wanted."

"We're supposed to believe something like this? Another one of your bizarre confessions?" Forrest's hands shake, a small droplet of sweat like a diver detaches itself from his forehead and plops into the middle of the paper. He is a heavy man in poor physical condition, probably suffering from tachycardia and sweats, Evans decides; not in any event the kind of man who would be able to understand the psychology of a superbly conditioned astronaut. "Impossible," Forrest says. "This is impossible."

"It's what I wanted to say."

"There are no creatures on Venus!" Forrest shouts, hurling a fist on the table, causing the frail paper of Evans' confession to jump slightly in place. "This is the foulest thing I have ever heard of in my life. We are not making progress but going backwards. Nothing has been accomplished."

"If that's so," Evans says mildly, "why don't you simply release me?"

"Don't give me any nonsense. If you want to know something, I'm beginning to lose patience with you. I'm finding it harder and harder to be professional; I think that you're doing this deliberately, that there's *perversity* in you, Evans. I have no patience for this, no tolerance. Things are moving entirely too quickly."

"I'm sorry," Evans says, crossing his legs, maintaining a superficial posture of ease before the damaged and distraught Claude Forrest. "I'm sorry that I've given you all these problems but I think you have to look beyond—"

"Are you serious about this? You'd have us believe this statement?"

"Why not?" Evans says and shrugs. He runs a hand across his forehead. "It's as good as anything else, isn't it? Just tell me what you want to hear and I'll work it out for you. I'm cooperative, genuinely cooperative. And besides that—"

"I'm sick of threatening you, Evans," Forrest says, standing. "I never thought that it would deteriorate into something like that. I thought that reasonable means would extract reasonable ends, but I was wrong. We won't be trifled with. There's too much at stake."

"May I have my statement back?" Evans says gently, reaching forward a hand, touching the paper, whisking it away from Forrest and curling it into his armpit. "There are some further things I'd like to add; perhaps I can change it around a bit; then too there's something else which—"

But he is able to say no more. Forrest reaches toward him, takes the paper from its nesting place, and pulls hard. The paper disintegrates: it shears into small, winding strips which burst from Forrest's hand, and flowering like crepe, fall from his palm, sinking toward the floor.

In that instant, looking at Forrest, Evans apprehends a still life: the paper arching like a small explosion pinned in the air, the shrouded eyes of Forrest staring at the paper; a look in his eyes halfway between woe and shock, reaching for the paper but unable to intercept it; his entire body convulsed toward that tissue as if by snatching it he could hold all of Evans in his hand and crush the sense out of him. But the eyes are already filled with defeat: he will never reach the paper, the paper is entirely beyond him, half-disintegrated and heading away, and in that moment Evans thinks that he understands the true nature of Forrest for the first time, not to say his role and his purposes, the small convulsions of intimidation and fear which must afflict him no less than any of the others, and Evans wants to reach forward and touch him, run a hand across his face in something approaching a caress, and say, "It's all right, it's all right," seeing Forrest then as a clumsy fat boy always somehow outside the center of his existence and only to come to grips with it through tears and rage; but as Evans reaches forward, trying to touch the stricken face of the psychiatrist, time seems to expire like a used reel of tape, which then clicks in the recorder and rewinds. Slowly, everything is played in reverse: the paper floats upward, Evans' hand retracts, Forrest backs away from him, and as always the strong, willing hands are there behind to seize the unfortunate Evans and drag him from the office, with only small kicks and squeals to indicate his protests. This is getting very repetitious. Everything is very much of a sameness here. There must be a way to break the cycle, to come free of those bonds: we need Venus, we must make Venus in this century; we have (we were advised) a great need for the potential living space, and then too there is no way that the program can survive if it does not have, later or sooner, one unalloyed triumph.

# 45

With clear apprehension I see myself on the *Kennedy II*; I am inside that ship, perhaps painted into one of the bulkheads or then again disguised (as my training would certainly make possible) as a piece of machinery, and from that vantage point, unspeaking, I can see the three astronauts detailed for the first expedition to Mars: there they are, just as I always remembered them, although not, of course, with the gloss of official portraiture to them; there they are, X, Y, and the captain, Z, deep in the capsule of the *Kennedy II*, burning fifteen million miles from earth, heading toward Mars, now sitting in a somewhat sullen crumple, mumbling to one another with the monitors off. They hope the monitors are off. They are told that there are no monitors on this flight, but on the other hand, they cannot be sure. There is very little for them to do because the flight is fully automated. Their first voluntary act will be a week from now—the opening of a hatchway so that Z and Y can step onto Mars—but that is a goodly distance in the future; it can hardly occupy them for all this time. Nor can the computations, the eating schedules, the checks of the support system. There are no television broadcasts to look forward to; in order to keep down public resistance the program wanted to make this flight with a minimum of publicity. Even so, there are supposed to have been small riots in the area of the launch on the day before lift-off. X, Y, and Z do not know very much about this. Y is something of a political theoretician but only *in absentia* and is ill-trained in the field. X and Z are simpler types.

It is politics that they are talking about now, or at least the politics of the program. Their conversation is quite desultory; there is no way that any of them can feign particular interest in his crewmates or the situation, but something must be done to pass the time; between the communications from the base, talk helps. Actually, Z is in the throes of a complex fear which he cannot ascertain; it is not exactly the matter of the landing and being the first man on Mars (the mission, they have been assured, is failsafe, and consider what happened to the first man on the moon) so much as it is some intricate sense of insufficiency: what is bothering Z at this moment is that he is not sure that he has any reason for being on this flight, that he in no way feels qualified to be the captain of the expedition, and that if not too many years ago he had made some zigs instead of zags in his life he would be in a far more favorable position today—lying in his own bed, watching foliage instead of dully clocking orbits in his head while the ship, now quite out of control, plunges toward Mars. It is this feeling which has led him to say, "Actually, I don't think that this is going to work out the way they hoped it would," and has sparked a discussion, in the throes of which all three of them are now.

"You're quite wrong," Y, the political theoretician, is saying, making hexagons in the air with a fist and using his other hand to support himself against a bulkhead, "it's the only way in which the program could be salvaged: by doing something really spectacular, going all the way to Mars. To reinaugurate the moon flights at this time would be a step backward—we'd be in the sixties' argument all over again—but this is unanswerable. Anyway, who knows? There may be gold deposits there." Y eases himself against a wall and shakes his head. "Such trepidation from the captain," he begins to say, thinking that he will draw some humorous parallel between Z's querulousness about the flight and the political opposition which the flight has generated, but something in the situation stops him, something he can see in Z's eyes and hands makes him realize that this will be a risky burlesque which might upset the cautious balance the crew has found in training and on the flight, and he stops, thinks about sealing off the discussion, then says, "Anyway, it doesn't matter. Isn't that right, X? Essentially, we're mechanics."

X, the youngest of the three, although in certain ways the most highly qualified (and the only one without a significant problem in his personal life: Y and his wife are working their way into a bitter divorce; Z's aged father, who has irreversible arteriosclerosis, has been living with his family for some seven years now, and his slow deterioration has brought at least two of Z's children to a point of serious emotional affliction, something that he went into with the program psychiatrist but that the psychiatrist did not think was serious enough to block his appointment, the aged father being at least photogenic in portraits and completely unaware of the changes which he had wrought upon family life), looks out a porthole and says, "It really isn't red after all. We'll have to look into that further. It must be our own atmosphere inducing spectral distortion. This is very interesting; they'll have to run some experiments."

But this routine scientific speculation seems to go beyond Y and Z. They are bound up in a different kind of metaphysic, other matters occupy them, and now, as I observe the scene on the *Kennedy II* closely (my vantage point not only allows me to apprehend everything which is going on but to distort or contract time as I will in order to arrive at the more interesting parts), it seems to be somewhat later; much later, in fact. It is now a sleep period, and as X sits impassively on the watch (they have decided that because of the asteroid belt or some other reason they had better keep a watch this time), his scientific eyes probing the mists of Mars, which appear more and more discolored as they approach, Y and Z, muttering, slump over themselves on their bunks. "Calculation, calculation!" Y cries in his sleep, and Z is saying "Dad, you've really got to cut this out. I can't stand looking at you any more; it's like a horrid joke," and "Save the situation," Y mumbles, and "For God's sake, doesn't the old bastard ever go to sleep?" says Z, and the intricate crosscurrent of dialogue continues: they are both heavy talkers, heavy sleeptalkers (maybe the effects of the ether are increasing their loquacity) and have much to say to their memories and themselves during sleep. X, hearing all of this, tries to ignore it; his burning, intense eyes sweeping the void before him. He is a scientific man, trained in anthropology and geological eras, who lives a cold and reserved life; unlike almost every other man who has come into the program fairly recently, he has made no distinction between his personal and his professional existence and therefore does not suffer from the tension and neurasthenia which so obviously affect his comrades. He will not listen to them, he resolves; he will have no part of their night thoughts; he has more interesting and sensible matters to resolve. What are the origins of Deimos and Phobos? Why the mathematical patterning of the old canals? Why the impression, in latter-day telescopy, of artifacts, monuments, erected on the sands? What does it mean? X exhales, thinks about artifacts, some shudder of mortality overtaking him as he wonders how he would feel if he were the man to find the first ruin of Mars. He cannot think upon it too long; he will remain in the capsule.

*I won't think of this any more,* X mutters, hunching his shoulders against the lively sleeptalking of his crewmates, trying to fixate his attention totally upon Mars. It is at that moment—I have been waiting for this for days—that I emerge from my hiding place on the *Kennedy II* and address myself to him for the first time. It means that I must lose something of my anonymity and hence safety, but then again there are certain things which I think it is absolutely necessary for me to tell X (who of the three is the only one for whom I can have hope, knowing what I know) at the present time. "Listen to me," I say, "you are the scientist, the mechanically inclined one, the only old-time realist on this flight. The other two are already descending under the strain. Hear me, hear me out. This flight is doomed and hopeless. You will never make Mars. You will for inexplicable reasons swing out from the presumed orbit and lurch into the asteroid belt. You will collide with Ceres and be pulverized. Nobody will ever be able to quite figure this out."

"That's interesting," X says, looking at his nails, "I've had the same fears myself. But there's nothing to be done about it. We'll win through."

"You cannot," I say. "You are doomed. It is 1981. All of this happened to you in 1976. It is five years later and you have become historical; the entire incident has already been put into the irretrievable frieze of archives, conferences, discussions, and books. You have less than forty-eight hours to live. All of you."

"This is not reasonable," X says. "I'm a reasonable man. You have no business getting near this unless you see certain things. Nothing you say can mean anything to me; you're talking about the imponderable."

"It's too late," I say. "Too late for argumentation. All of this happened a long time ago. We can only regard it in retrospect. So tell me. Why? Why did it happen?"

"Nothing happened," X says, his color breaking sharply. With the omnipotence I have been able to register as a stowaway upon this historical flight, I deduce that his pulse rate shows elevation to 106. His blood pressure is now 150/91, a significant alteration. Small pineal secretions dart like squid through his bloodstream and produce a reflexive stirring in the groin; his genitals retract. Emerge. Retract. "Nothing happened," he says, "nothing will happen. The flight will be completed successfully. We will make certain observations of Mars and return five weeks from today. Four weeks, six days, and twelve hours. Receptions are planned. We will be received in the major cities."

"No," I say remorselessly, impatience now edging past the compassion that I want to feel. "That is not the way it happened."

"Ah, God," Y says in his sleep, "the calculations are all wrong. There's no percentage." He stirs thickly, moves to a precipice of consciousness, then moves under somnolence again. "No percentage."

"Get out of here," X says to me. "You're not permitted on board. Only authorized personnel—"

"I'm authorized," I say. "It is 1976. In five years, although I do not know this yet, I will be the copilot on the first expedition to Venus. I have already joined the program. I have passed fitness and security tests. I have a right to be here. A right to be here."

"No," X says, moving back to a bulkhead and taking from it a large wrench, one which has been casually dangling throughout our conversation. It is there for emergency adjustment of superficial screws and bolts, should that be needed, but X, Y, and Z have not even been properly instructed in its use. "I won't have it; I won't listen to this any more. Get out of here."

"You will miss the orbit of Mars," I say earnestly, gesturing, trying to explain to him before he does something disastrous. Perhaps X is the wrong person to speak with. I would have done better with the more analytical Y, the subtler and more tormented Z, if I had only waited for an appropriate time. But my schedule is limited, I am controlled by forces no less onerous than those which shape the flight (I am not, legally speaking, entitled to be aboard at all, and the time factor is damaging), and I must do what I can with X, who as he regards me, now palpating the wrench in his hands, seems less and less capable of reason. "You will splinter into Ceres and be totally demolished. Instrumentation and monitoring will reveal nothing. It is a mystery, a complete mystery as to how this could have happened. Scientists will be dismayed, politicians shamed, the public either pleased or querulous, depending upon their point of view. It will be laid, eventually, to computer error, although everybody at the higher echelons will know that this is a lie. The computers have never malfunctioned. Families will be bereaved, officials at the highest level of the political structure will be possessed by terror. The program will be virtually abandoned. Moon stations will be shut down. Jobless, men will return from capsules to the earth. A national day of mourning will be decreed, but even that will merely heighten the tension. Plans will be made and then rapidly abandoned for a second expedition to Mars. Unmanned probes will be sent forth almost capriciously, without scheduling and preparation, and one by one will all miss the target. Those politicians in all the major parties who are against the continuation of the program will have a seeming triumph, and the program will be nearly repudiated. Ceremonies of remembrance will be held in many cities. The program, shattered, will have to recoup by becoming invisible; it will be possible for the program to continue only through a reversal of all those devices which have brought it to this point. Preparations for the Venus flight will be made under blackout; monies for financing will be diverted from other appropriations. There will be no publicity. An onerous training program, painful and terrible, will begin for the two men who will go to Venus. A certain air of desperation will infest the preparations for this flight. The program will move forward, although it does not want to admit this, in the implicit assumption that it cannot touch Venus and that the flight will be a disaster. Nevertheless, and nevertheless . . ."

"No," X says, "no, I can't take this any more." He poises, his face assumes a plodding and earnest expression; he swings the wrench at me. I try to duck but am too slow, too caught up in my own dialogue, to retain reflexes and take a shattering blow on the scalp, no, it is the temple, the cheekbone, the occipital range in the back of the head, the medulla oblongata, the tissues of the medulla splitting, blood rising, lymph drooling, bone dripping, and my head flies apart, I collapse before X, the last thing which my destroyed vision apprehends is the wrench, now moving out of the peripheral range, being carried by X, to another part of the ship. "Dirty sons of bitches; I'll kill them all!" X screams and then I hear bone shattering again, whimpers and moans from surprised beds and then thankfully no more, no more, I slide over the edge and am gone from the flight although not, unhappily or at least for a time, from life itself, which continues as it must, ever reaching toward the Unknown.

# 46

The novel that I will write telling the full and final truth of the Venus expedition progresses. Now I believe that I have found a form for it, a true fit, a raison d'être: I will be able to apprehend the truth because throughout the whole sweep and scope of the book there will not be a single moment, a passage so precise and detailed that I will have to come to grips with myself and my true relation to the Captain. That is the difficult part; the rest of it I can handle: I know of the magnitudes of stars, calculations of windages, intricacies which will enable the computers one by one to release all of their deadly secrets; only upon the personal aspects am I, by virtue of inferior training, slightly weak. So we will dodge, in the novel, the issue of myself, the issue of the Captain; we will instead write sixty-seven chapters—I think of the novel as having many chapters, some of them interlocking, others never seeming to fit at all; a crazy dazzle this, but I am no novelist—and in some of them I will show myself at work and in others I will show my friend Evans at play and in still others perhaps we will deal with the Captain fucking, the Captain breathing, the objective history of the voyage, but in none of them, absolutely none of them at all, will I have to bear down upon the personal, and thus the secret slowly by slow piece by piece will be revealed: that in none of it, when the truth is finally known, was there anything personal. None of it was ever personal at all: it was merely a question of machinery, intersection, causality, orbits. The working of the ship against the firmament; the slow, chuckling conversations which the computers had with themselves. But nothing. Nothing personal. Nothing of that at all: we have been trained well; now there is nothing left to reveal. All of it has been squeezed out midway between Venus and the sun, the pieces of ourselves that might have told the truth all squeezed in the compression chamber, knifed down and now gnarled upon themselves like little entrails.

I really should get started on the novel. My time here is not —although it often seems so—unlimited; sooner or later the cycle will end and I will have to do other things. It would be nice to emerge with the novel. I truly will begin upon it soon, but minor elements of the characterization are still troubling me and will have to be carefully worked out. I am taking notes. I am preparing myself. I am getting ready. It is merely a question of a block, a tiny little block, laying like a sword across the brain; soon enough or sooner I will break it and then soon to work. *Beyond Apollo*, by Harry M. Evans: a true and real study of the space program from the history of its inception to the present day. It will be one hundred and thirty-eight pages long. As has been the custom with my forebears from the program who have published books (but mine, aha, mine will not be ghostwritten!), I will get an agent to make the very best deal for me, but I will keep a careful and a cunning hand upon all of the subsidiary rights.

# 47

A brief history of the solar system. The solar system was created in 1951 when a massive series of cosmic gases created by the explosion and disintegration of the *previous* solar system finally congealed to create its aspect much as we know it today. There were ten planets, one of which, Luna, midway between Terra and Mars, due to improper alignment of the planets swerved out of orbit, plunged into Terra, and in the ensuing explosion became permanently fixed as the satellite of that minor planet. In 1952 atmospheres were fixed on the five inner planets and the first signs of primordial life began to ooze from the still-boiling seas of Terra, the only planet upon which the existence of intelligent life has been verified to date. These elements took their first trembling foothold upon the land in 1953, the same year that the New York Yankees defeated the Brooklyn Dodgers in the World Series, despite the gallant efforts of the Dodgers' pitcher Carl Erskine, who won two games. In 1954, equipped with respiratory passages and the first flickers of purposeful mentality, these forms began to set up primitive means of living on the land and in 1955 and 1956 the highest of the higher forms began to live in clearly defined societies, establish taboos, and create artifacts for the purpose of survival and slaughter. In 1957, the same year that the first sputnik went into orbit before an astonished world, these forms were making their first step toward civilization and the creation of technology; this technology, largely refracted through religion, was responsible for the rapid growth of the species through the late 1950's and the corollary diminution and entrapment of most of the subspecies on the planet. In 1961 certain obscure events associated with religiosity resulted in the overthrow of one culture, the establishment of a much wider series of cultures holding similar tenets, and the exclusion of yet other groups which resulted in a polarization among this most intelligent species, one which has yet to be fully explained. In 1962 and 1963, as Kennedy was being assassinated and planning to invade Cuba, a network of interdependent civilizations was created and the largest amount of the land surface was prepared for technological exploitation; in 1965 poets, artisans, musicians, and priests combined with the technologically trained to produce massive systems of machinery and commerce that further utilized the resources of the planet. Technology was commercialized and a large proportion of the species began to feel a certain sense of displacement between themselves and the products of their work in 1966, the very same year that the Orioles knocked off the Dodgers four straight in the World Series (the age of space travel was inaugurated in the late 1960's); in 1970 the first primitive shots and probes moving from the planet; by 1973 primitive means of space flight had been devised, the same year that the Cardinals took it all; and the first manned flight to the moon occurred in 1975, the famous first words of the explorer on the moon being beamed back instanteously to all of the population on Terra; in the late 1970's, as the dominance of the Detroit Lions over the world of professional football seemed unbreakable, flights were made toward Mars; and then in 1981 the first expedition to Venus was devised and it was at that time the solar system ended. Massive if inexplicable cosmic forces caused it to implode and come to a fiery culmination: including the planets of Mercury, Venus, Terra, Mars, Jupiter and many famous others. The solar system was reconstituted in 1993 and again in 2035, but at the present time we are unable to chronicle the stages of its history through those incarnations.

# 48

"Because of a blind series of events," I say to the Captain, only slightly disconcerted after the Fourth Great Venusian Disturbance. "All of it is coincidence, causality, blind alleys, the manufacturing of explanations after the fact for any one of an infinite series of possibilities which have no origin whatsoever. We had reached a point in our technological spectrum where a flight to Venus was inevitable; therefore it was made. Past that fact there is no explanation whatsoever. So it falls to us to invent, post facto, an explanation which will seem credible; we will tie the meaning to the event, as it were, rather than the event to the meaning, because that is the kind of people we are. So the reason that we are going to Venus—"

"No," the Captain says, raising his hand. His eyes are deep, pained, solemn; he too seems to be suffering from aftereffects of the Great Venusian Disturbance, although with some difficulty he is holding himself together. "I'm sorry. I can't allow that. You've gone way over fifty words."

"Oh," I say, somewhat shamed. "All right, I have. But it isn't easy—"

"You must do it in less than fifty words," the Captain says. He leans forward, the crinkles of his face as deep and cold as the valleys of the moon. "Those are the rules. But I will tell you this. I will admit this. You are showing progress; you are getting somewhat closer now, and perhaps there is hope for you after all. Perhaps I will be able to confess everything. But now I can say no more, say no more at all," he adds and settles back. I put my hand to my chin, finger to lips, and ponder all the myriad ways that I can phrase what I have just said to him more concisely, but it is difficult, difficult: the game becomes more challenging as the answer becomes closer; and the Great Venusian Disturbance, replete with rich and final images of the Captain's death as they took their leave, has been highly unsettling. It is hard to intellectualize. It is harder and harder to intellectualize. The Captain giggles and runs his hands over his thighs: perhaps he is already anticipating the many dirty stories he will be able to tell me when first I solve my puzzle.

"Give me time, give me time," I say (not knowing whether I mean to address the Venusians or the Captain) and try to formulate the best way of putting what I think, perhaps (but then again one may always be wrong) what I already know so well.

# 49

In the night I dream again that Forrest comes alone into my room, a curious state of mournfulness coming from him, and sits to talk. He places himself on the one chair in this room, leans his head over his knees, looks at the walls, runs his eyes over and past me. Now, seeing him in dishabille, I realize for the first time that he is old: not my age at all, but at least ten and maybe twenty years older; obese and puffing now from the effort to keep himself from sliding into total physical disintegration. "I don't know," he says, "I don't know, we've tried everything. Everything. And it doesn't work. I'm highly qualified. I know more about the psychology of space than any man who has ever lived. I devised the training program, the control systems, the checks and balances. And now . . ."

"It's all right," I say, realizing that he needs for me to respond in that way. "It isn't your fault."

"I thought I understood everything. All of it was correlated to the maximum; there was no possibility of error. It wasn't too big, too frightening; it was completely routine. I showed them that. I built this program. Almost by myself I built it."

"Don't worry."

"All of the factors were calculated. Men would perform in space as they performed in any stressful situation. There was no difference in the calculations, the preparations. I staked my life and reputation on it."

"It couldn't have been done better," I assure him. "You did an excellent job."

"I was responsible for Mars as well. Mars was the first mission on which I worked closely. I had everything charted out and then look at what happened."

"You couldn't know. You couldn't be involved."

"But I said, what the hell, the hell with Mars; it was a bad situation. Computer error; a failure of orbits. It was the mathematics of the situation which broke down, not the psychology. I was not a humble man!" Forrest says passionately. "I was not a man for having second thoughts! I believed in rigor, order, logic, and control, and converted these beliefs into my own self-assessment. When the time came for Venus, I was positive that it would work. Hadn't it always worked? I knew that it would work. It was fine in the simulator."

"Yes," I say earnestly, "you did an excellent job of preparing for us; you couldn't help it if there turned out to be Venusians after all and if the Captain—"

"But then everything seemed to break down." I realize that Forrest is weeping. It is really quite disgraceful for him to be in such a reduced condition and I am embarrassed for the man, but what can I do? I put my hands on his shoulders, turn him toward me— almost as if I were beginning the gentlest of embraces—and then hold him over my shoulder, letting the sobs rack through him and by implication through me. I am not crying. I am moved but not disconcerted; I always knew that beyond it all, Forrest was this way.

"The simulations were very fatiguing," I say. "They made us vomit and become impotent. For days afterward they would give us a frail hold on consciousness: like an old man holding onto a stick, seeing the sidewalk slide away from him, we felt as if consciousness might depart or turn over on us at any moment, but that made us strong for the voyage. And the cold sweats and the feelings of dread which we had all the time after the early simulations, those were good too because they reduced the universe to another spell of neurasthenia. You did a fine job. You had our best interest at heart."

"I want to believe that," Forrest says. "Oh, how I wanted you to say that, to know that you understood: I never wanted to do anything *bad* to you; we merely had to get you in the best possible condition for the *voyage,* that was all; and now I have people saying that I didn't do my job and somehow it was my fault. It *wasn't* my fault; don't you see how hard I'm trying to cure you?" Forrest says and then he quite loses control, seems to collapse over me: I am strangled by his weight, his enormous ballooning weight lies over me like ice, like death, like blankets of fire, and try as I may, I cannot seem to get free of him; Forrest is over me now, Forrest's weeping face searching the ceiling and then my eyes, up and down he moves, over and out, I cannot get free, he moves up and down on top of me; I realize that Forrest is trying to screw me, it has always been intended that way, this was always lying at the heart of our relationship, and I try even more frantically to get away, but he is insensate, mad, quite gone into his psychiatric necessity, and even through layers of clothing and sheets I can feel his uncoiling prick moving toward me with deadly efficiency. *Oh!* Forrest moans. *Ah!* and somehow accomplishes an entrance: now at last it has happened; he has penetrated me, a man has penetrated me, not the Captain (which in a way I always wanted) but Forrest, who has come to discover the Cap-

103

tain, and some mad asepsia in me wants him at the least not to stain the sheets and thus leave evidence, but asepsia be damned, circumstances be damned, Forrest is pumping on me, moving like a fat rabbit (is it possible that I looked this way over my wife? how do women stand it?) and with a scream, a whooping cry of love Forrest discharges himself into or against me (it is hard to tell, everything is so tumbled together) and then, spent, lies against me moaning. *Catalepsy,* he says, *cataleptic breakdown, schizo-effective psychosis, ideas of reference, hallucinatory impact,* and although he is still moaning in pain one wise, dreadful eye, peering above me, seen without his knowledge, seems to regard everything with irony and implication, and I suspect—although I can not be sure of this—that this has been one more Technique to get the Truth from me and now, pleased with his efficacy if somewhat doubtful of the results, Forrest is merely reviewing certain aspects of his training so that in the morning, as ever, he can remember that he was a professional and that everything he did was only for business' sake.

# 50

HELEN EVANS

LENA H SNEEV

ALE SHEEVL

LENEH VENAS

"Come," I say to Leneh Venas, taking her hand as I did a long time ago before the program taught me the true uses of sentiment, "come with me; I'll show you Venus," and we arch forward, high and far, moving without benefit of rocketry toward the green planet which shrouded in its gases lies at first above and then below us as we move in more closely.

"It's beautiful," she says, holding me more closely and taking cautious peeks over my shoulder at the aspect of the planet; I can feel her hand moving up and down the panes of my back, just a suggestion of contact in it, the absent-minded sexuality of women, something attached to them of which they are often not even conscious. I feel my back arch, a stir of response, but unshielded in the void is no place for physical dalliance. "Beautiful," she says again as we circle in toward the planet for a closer look. "Is it real?"

"Yes," I say, "it's scientifically proven to be the second planet from the sun."

"I don't believe in planets," Leneh Venas says, holding my hand. "I never told you this before because I thought that you would laugh at me, but I think the whole thing is made up. Planets and stars and constellations; they're just something pasted over the sky which we imagine. Actually, it's just us and then they have to make up names and explanations for these things or otherwise there would be an investigation."

"It's true," I say, "it's been verified."

"Oh, I know they *tell* us it's true," Leneh says with a small laugh, "but how do we really know? It's hard to be a scientific wife and have all your illusions taken from you. That's the real thing I couldn't forgive you, you know. The other reasons were just made-up bullshit. I couldn't stand all that factuality. Is there anything alive down there?"

"I don't know," I say, peering with her through the gases; seeing small gray shapes whisking in and out of the line of vision. We are very close to Venus now, some five hundred miles or less above the planet and the thin, high scent of the atmosphere causes our ears to ring, although we seem otherwise to be doing very well without breathing apparatus or shielding of any sort. Perhaps we could have withstood space travel all the time; it was only our inert sense of caution which made things so difficult. "Do you care for me, Leneh Venas?" I ask her, putting an affectionate arm around her shoulders, letting my fingers ease down to her breast as the two of us, five hundred miles high, look at the green and gaseous planet. "Do you?"

"Well," she says, "you took me on this interesting trip and have shown a lot of concern for me. I think that's nice."

"But do you love me? That's the question which I asked you."

"Well," she says with a laugh, her fingers catching mine and drawing them subtly toward an arched nipple. "Love is very hard to decide. This is just our first date, you know. You have to give these things time."

"But could you love me?"

"Maybe," she says with a giggle, "and maybe not, but probably maybe," and detaches herself from me, makes a little girl's twist of her body, and smiling, sinks toward the planet, I make swimming gestures and find that I can follow her easily, the ozone supporting me; a strange and invigorating feeling of buoyancy working itself through various levels of the body. Interplanetary travel in this fashion is excellent; when the solar system is invented again they will have to try that alternative. "I have to tell you something, Leneh Venas," I say, catching up with her near a cloud formation, the cloud orange and shaped somewhat like a child's stuffed animal, "I hope that something can develop between us because I've been very hurt. I was married once, you know."

"I heard something about that," she says vaguely, extending an arm so that I can float against her, then gathering me in and running her fingers down a forearm. "You don't have to talk about that. Isn't this pretty? It's hard to believe that Venus is something made up when you see it like this."

"It isn't made up."

"Well, if it isn't, it *could* be," she says. "Let's not talk of that."

"I was once married," I say. "That's what I was talking about. It was very unhappy. It was terrible. She understood nothing and it came apart in pity and terror. She left me, and in doing so, denied everything."

"I'm sorry," she says. "It's very common nowadays, isn't it? People not understanding each other. Let's not talk about it. Let's just enjoy the day and let what will happen happen."

"But we can't," I say, recalling something, remembering the conditions under which we have been permitted to make this voyage. "We can only go for a little while and then we have to come back. And we have to reach some kind of a resolution, Leneh. We have to decide between ourselves today what will become of us. It's a decision."

"That's so tiring," she says, shaking her head. "I can't make any decisions. I just want to look at Venus and dream that it's real. Can't we do that?"

"No," I say and exert pressure on her: it pains me to do so but I dig my fingers into her ribs, make her eyes widen with an *oh!* of surprise, draw her into me, see comprehension beginning to filter through her cheekbones as if poured from a vial somewhere above. "We can't do that: we have to reach a decision today. Right now, in fact."

"I don't even know you."

"You have to know me. You have to take risks, make judgments. That's what they wanted—"

"No," she says, shaking her head, not withdrawing her eyes from me. "I can't do that. If that's what they want, they'll have to find you someone else because I can't be rushed like that. I don't know—"

"You've got to know," I say. The cloud dissolves convulsively under us; I find myself suddenly in an uncomfortable position. Pinned against her, arms and legs now awkwardly intertwined, we are falling rapidly toward Venus. "You've got to make a decision," I say as thick, foul currents of atmosphere in the lower regions begin to sicken me, giving my head a stuffed sensation. "You can't live this way all your life. You have got to come to the point. Do you—"

"No," she says, crying, "I don't understand you; I don't understand any of you, you're all the same, all that you want are immediate decisions, easy answers, and there are none: you have to let some things develop, take their time, get away from me," shrieking out all of this in sudden bubbles of sound as we fall and fall. Now we are approaching the land; it appears to be a thick, gaseous, vile swamp, not at all like the Venus of which I have dreamed and without signs of intelligent life as well, although strange convulsions and twitches of the mud beneath indicate that there may be large beasts in hiding. "Nothing, nothing; it can't be that way," Leneh Venas says, and falls away from me; her body detaches fully and bones seem to break; she is coming apart, head flying from the neck, shoulders from joints, joints from trunk; and I am falling toward Venus, completely out of control and surrounded by a constellation of human anatomy, all broken and spattered with blood. "You can't do this to me!" I cry, just before I hit the swamp, "you cannot possibly do this to me; it's not allowed, it isn't fair!" but then the dismembered body of Leneh Venas and I, the two of us—both of us, that is to say—come to land with an unseemly roar and topple; smiling, the beasts pad from their groves to devour us, and therefore it is difficult to say if we were able to make much out of our relationship or whether, in the long run, we were able to work out some kind of meaningful emotional interconnection.

# 51

"Ridiculous," I say to my dead uncle, who seems to be keeping me company in the ship on the way back after the unfortunate end of the Captain, "it's absolutely ridiculous. Nothing like this can work out. Impossible. Impossible."

"Struggle," he croaks. He seems to be in a state of dishabille; his face is ashen, he has lost a great deal of weight; possibly even after death the disease has decided to have another bite of him. "Achievement. Testing. Sacrifice. Where there's a will."

"It can't work," I say. "Nothing like this can work. Sooner or later they have to face that."

"Onward. Outward and inward. Ever voyaging. A quitter never quits. A winner never wins. The game fish leap the draw-bridge. Only the mightiest oak ever knew stone."

"Because if they don't face it we're going to lose the solar system time and again. Just like before. They've gone at it the wrong way. It's impossible."

"Never sew a needle. A stitch in darkness brings the light. Making tall the tower never brought home the bacon. Into the cloven jaws of victory. Pardon me, son," my dead uncle says. "I seem to be somewhat ill. Could you give me a hand?" He stands, sways under the fluorescence of the ship, stares blankly at the portholes. "Maybe you'd just better eject me," he says softly. "I'd just be ballast now. Dispose of me and on your way. No reason for me to hold up your progress."

"No progress," I say. I seem to be in a rather florid state, although I am not quite sure at this moment what I am driving at, however intensely. "Only the same darkness forever repeated. On a different scale. I couldn't possibly jettison you."

"Why not? What's done is needed and—"

"You're a relative."

"All the more reason. Sentimentality cannot hold us back. Oh, my boy," my uncle says, his face turning a vivid green, rais-ing a transluscent hand to cover his mouth, "I am very ill. I tried to conceal this knowledge but. Cannot do this. Out the porthole." He staggers toward an opening, leans against glass; I can see his body outlined against the stars. "No need for this any more," he whispers, and makes feeble efforts to open the glass.

"No," I say, "not that way. There's an exit hatchway you can use if you must." I do not want him to leave me, but on the other hand, even in this extremity I respect my uncle and do not want him to suffer the indignity of being balked. "This way," I say and take his thin hand, feel his wasted flesh, lead him toward the exit trap. It is open, still warm from the recent use put to it by the Captain, still reeking faintly of his own fluids. "In here," I say to my uncle and pick him up very easily by the scruff of his neck and deposit him in the exit chute. With small murmurs and moans of gratitude he sinks within it like a puppy, curls around himself.

"Yes," he says, "yes, yes, far better this way. Onward toward the stars. Ever hopeful. Into the expansion. Struggle and sacrifice. Inward and outward," and so on until I realize that he has no more to tell me and so in a spirit of selflessness I close the chute, pushing it all the way to the wall, and set the buttons on automatic. There is a small hiss, like the first time, and my uncle disappears into the void. I am becoming proficient. I am becoming proficient.

For a while in the empty humming ship it seems that I am still accompanied by him; as, attracted by my gravity, his body works out small mad arcs and circlets in the void, and now and then a small phrase burbles through: "accomplishment," I hear, "striving," "struggle," and so on, but this is nonsense; my uncle is decomposed and deep into the ether and there is no way that he can talk to me ever again. After a time the voice goes away, the sounds tumble into night; we shriek back toward earth at ten accelerating miles a second, where with or without his help I will have to deliver the news, breaking it to them gently, of course, and with enough dissimulation that for at least a while they will think I am mad . . . and I can lead them thus ever so gently into understanding.

# 52

"It's working. I think it's working," I hear someone (probably Forrest) say, but when I look up it is only at the familiar ceiling and I know that nothing is working at all.

# 53

Pawn to king four leads inevitably into the Ruy Lopez and the pawn sacrifice at the eighth move, but at the seventh move West sees the ploy and trumps over overtrick, thereby losing a rook but putting the ace of trumps into a menacing position; it is then necessary to castle, thereby losing two tricks in the process but setting up a situation where the unblocked queen will be able to make a preemptive no-trump overcall, therefore working out the spade king before it can capture the pawn. I am right. The system will definitely work if I can only keep the code. The code is sure and unswerving; it has to do with the unblinking acceptance of all possibilities, the institutionalization of passion, the willingness to understand that any of it, all of it, can be reduced to a simple binary code which when placed upon a strip of tape will summarize everything, all of it being binary at best and binary sometimes putting the best interpretation on it. Alone, always alone, leading the heart king to the exposed bishop will inevitably result in an undertrick if I do not pass the pawn into West's finessed heart queen and his jack of knights.

# 54

*A Brief History of the Universe:* The universe was invented by man in 1976 as a cheap and easy explanation for all of his difficulties in conquering it. "We must turn our eyes earthward and no longer think of the universe," politician C said in a famous speech four days after the failure of the Mars expedition to reach its predestined goal. "A nation, a world that is capable of appropriating such sums of money for the conquest of the universe should be able to feed the hungry, congeal the sick, want the needy before it can turn its eyes starward in the vainglorious pursuit of the unknown. I say that our universe is within," politician C said, whereupon politicians D, L, and M made similar statements, and M presented a long position paper in which he proved that it was the universe which was responsible for all of his difficulties in reaching a constituency and it was therefore time to move from the universe to less abstract and more immediate needs. As a result of this famous paper politician M was able to seek and attain high national office, although until long past the election politician C claimed that all of it had been appropriated from him and that he, politician C and not M, was responsible for the realignment in thinking and priorities. "Nevertheless, I will not desist," C said, "I will not desist from the brave and lonely battle to convince men that they can no longer think of the universe but must think of themselves."

Counter-theories indicate that the universe had been invented earlier, perhaps as early as 1941, in order to control the political situation in one of the parent countries at this time. "The enemy is the scourge of the universe!" it was said at this earlier date of history, "and we must save the universe from him!" It is also suggested that the universe was invented in 1950, 1951, and 1965, but the final date of 1976 is rendered as genuinely authentic, and there has been little dispute on the higher levels as to the fact that this date is correct.

The universe is composed of all the known and unknown galaxies and as per the theories of Einstein is thought to be infinite in a finite and curved fashion. There are several hundred known galaxies and it is estimated that there are several million more which have not yet been catalogued. Each of the galaxies contains at least one million stars, more than half of which are presumed to have planetary systems. Some of the stars, such as Antares, are so large that our entire solar system could be placed several times over within its present orbits. Others such as the dwarf star Rigel are little larger than the planet Terra, although of course somewhat hotter. Stars are in a constant process of ascent and decline and their life cycle can be measured in several billion years. Despite this, during any given Terran year several million stars expire either in nova, supernova, or cosmic accident due to the final consumption of all their potential heat sources.

It was this universe which was invented in 1976. Prior to then there had been no final explanation for the difficulties on the planet Terra. This universe superseded the older concept of the galaxy, which had been invented circa 1920, and the stars, authenticated to have been invented in 1891. The whole world theory, which had been invented five hundred years or more before the stars, had long since been discredited, of course, and bears no relation to the present brief discussion.

"The universe itself reels in its path and cannot sleep when these children go hungry," politician M added in 1977, causing the program to burrow even further underground, further from the public line of sight, where to this day it still exists, coalescing around the firm but slightly collapsed body of Evans, who prepares these conceptualizations for future generations. "The children" to whom politician M referred are no longer, most of them, hungry, having been the object of reappropriated funds from the dwindling accounts of the program, but this is not to say that all of them are sated; some of them are sated, but on the other hand, some of them are dead.

# 55

"You see," the Captain says in the aftermath of the Fourth Disturbance, "they make the case very clearly. It's either both of us or you. If it's both of us, no one returns, and if it's you, then I return to tell the tale and to warn them to stay away. So you have to understand that I'm not being selfish. It isn't me against you; that's the alternative they presented me with. Both or you."

"That's interesting," Evans says. "The way they told it, it was both of us or *you*. They thought that it would make more sense to finish off the senior man. More frightening, you understand, more final."

"Well," the Captain says, somewhat shakily readjusting his clothing, patting his hands up and down his buttocks to assure, as it were, their continued stolidity, "one of us is lying then. It was very definitely *you* they said they would have disposed of. Of course, if you don't believe me—"

"Maybe they told us different things. We got different communications."

"No," the Captain says, shaking his head, "that's impossible. It was very definite what they said and I couldn't possibly have made a mistake, so it's very definite what has to be done now." He continues patting his buttocks, retreats to a bulkhead, picks up an emergency wrench. "Here," he says, brandishing it, small wickers of starlight from the open ports bouncing off the wrench, "this is it. I'm going to have to kill you, Evans."

"Oh, no," I say, "there's nothing like that at all. *They* said they would take care of it." Nevertheless, I retreat, my respiration somewhat faster, looking hastily at the control board to see if there is anything which I myself can use. There are a few bolt heads, a couple of testing devices, but nothing so efficacious as a wrench. It occurs to me that for all his stupidity the Captain is cunning and dangerous. "Stop it," I say, having gone as far as I can, feeling the hard ridges of the console digging into the small of my back. "Stop it now."

"I can't stop it, Evans. I'm under very specific orders to kill you. I was told that by certified Venusians and I don't care to argue with them. Or with you, for that matter; the time for discussions is behind us. Come here, Evans, let me hit you on the head. It will just be a simple tap, nothing painful at all, and then it will be done. Consider that you're doing it for your country."

"No," I say. The survival instinct seems to have been well nurtured by the program's training; in any event, it is clearly stronger than I thought it might have been. "No," I say again and for lack of anything else pick up a discarded computer tape lying crosswise across one of the spools. It is not strong but it is resilient, and I might be able to strangle the Captain.

"Come here," he says again, closing the distance between us, "come here and I'll tell you everything you wanted to know about my sex life. After all, you never had the chance to hear everything. Here's your opportunity, Evans: I'll tell you it all. I first fucked when I was fourteen and if you want to know the truth, it was with a pig, but at least it was a female; the way it was—"

But I have been one stumbling step ahead of the Captain's mad cleverness; as he has been talking he has lifted the wrench to shoulder position, then feinted with it as if to tuck it under his arm and then at the moment when he felt I would have been entrapped and absorbed by his revelation of the pig the wrench is raised, the wrench moves toward my temple . . . but cunning in my own madness and with the advantage of emotional control on my side (the Captain is absorbed in his recollection of the sow), I spin toward him, raise a foot gracelessly, recollect several defensive moves that we were taught in the program against the possibility of aliens, and catch him midway in the thigh, follow to the solar plexus with a recurring kick (I have a certain delicacy about the area of the groin), and watch while the Captain falls heavily, still mumbling about fucking the pig. "I really loved that pig," the Captain says. "She was the only living being who was ever truly mine; then I got involved in relationships and everything got fucked up." All the fight, it seems, has gone out of him; I take the wrench gently from his hand (he slides it toward me with an almost collaborative leer, still talking about the pig) and I take it, tap him once lightly in the occipital zone. Immediately the hemorrhaging begins; small veins appear and burst in the Captain's face; a glow overtakes and then vanishes from his cheeks; and one cold eye, lifeless and wise, stares up at me as the other one closes effortlessly, sealing the Captain off for all time from any question of an existence which can simultaneously contain pigs and love.

Grunting, I pick him up; grunting, I carry him to the disposeway; (there is love in the way I do this; at last I am able to express the tender feelings I have always had for him without shame; my palm grazes his groin, my cheek rubs against his moist unshaven neck), and delicately I place him in there, patting the Captain into place; then I commit upon him a final, unspeakable act (which I will never, never tell) and close the hatchway, root the handle into place, and start the process of eviction and evisceration. I stand watching all of this so that I will be able to tell the tale well. I have been appointed by the Venusians to carry out these tasks and being in their horrible clutches, the least I can do is to remember them well.

I have not done these deeds myself; the Venusians have taken over my mind and have made me do it. On my own I could never have done anything to the Captain. I loved the Captain and admired him as well; took from him strengths which I would not have possessed otherwise, learned many things from him and felt that I had much more to learn. But I had no choice. I had no choice.

The machinery whirs. It is ready for evacuation. I press a relay. Like a small packet of feces, the Captain is hurled out into the universe, hitting the ether with a terrific roar which—surrounded as I am by thousands and thousands of miles of compressed plastic and tubing—I cannot hear. I hear nothing. All that I hear are the voices of the Venusians telling me "well done, well done," praises for my dedication and efficiency; and small thunderlike handclaps breaks over me as I wearily pick up the wrench and head back toward the console to perform my small and bitter tasks. I will have to break the news of the Captain. I will have to figure out a way to control the overrides to get the ship home. I will have to ascertain some manner in which I can please the Venusians while at the same time not striking the debriefing staff as being incurably insane. Much to do, much to do: but my entire training in the program has prepared me to do cheerfully hard, unrewarding work and so I will do it, do it, do it . . .

# 56

In the night I think that I hear the voices of the Venusian Disturbance again. I hope that this is not true; I have had no contact with them since return, but indisputably the sounds are familiar, the torments and twitches of consciousness are something which I have undergone before. I try to burrow under sleep, understand that I cannot do this, struggle out of unconsciousness slowly, extruding first one part of me and then another until I am at a kind of attention. "Please," I say. "I've been reasonable. Don't bother me any more."

"I'm sorry, Evans," the voices say. "We are not pleased. Your efforts are not credible."

"What more would you have me do? I've done every single thing possible."

"No, you haven't. You've done exactly what you wanted to do and then rationalized it that way. We are not happy, Evans. Not at all."

"Maybe I was wrong," I say. "I can admit that. Maybe I got into the program for the wrong reasons. I never thought too much about it; it was just the largest challenge I could find, but I don't know why I wanted challenges. None of this can be answered."

"None of your rationalizations, Evans," the voices say. "We are unspeakably, totally uninterested in personal data. You are of no concern to us at all. We are interested only in what you do. It is not satisfactory. The job is not being done."

"I've tried," I say. "Consider the difficulties." I try to keep my voice low: I have done many things in this room since I came here, committed many bizarre acts indeed, but one thing I have not been detected doing, at least until this moment, has been conducting earnest dialogues with myself. I cannot afford this. "Consider the difficulties," I murmur. My throat is dry. I cough up phlegm to moisten my throat, find that I am choking, bury my coughs under the pillow. Nothing seems to work out right.

"They are thinking of going back," the voices say. "We happen to know this; our sources are good. They are not through with Venus and they think you are being perverse. A theory has been developed which places the blame completely upon you and enables them to think of another expedition. We cannot tolerate this."

"I've told them the truth," I say. "I've always tried to tell them the truth."

"They have decided that you went mad on the voyage, killed the Captain, and then disposed of his body. Then somehow were able to take over the computers and come back. They blame you wholly for the problem. They admit no other involvement."

"I tried," I say. "I tried."

"We do not want you people coming toward our planet again," the voices say. "This is a final warning. We will not discuss this with you again, Evans: you are not worth our time. If there is another instance, we will have to take drastic action. Cosmic actions. We destroyed your planet once, you know; we can do it again very easily."

"But why," I say, "why does this all bear down on me? I have nothing to do with it. I have had nothing to do with it all along; I was just the man aboard. Why am I in the middle?"

"That's your problem."

"Don't you understand how tired I am of all this?" I say. It is the first time that I have ever tried to explain my position and my doing so to the voices of the Disturbance is probably complete misplacement, but nevertheless, somehow I too am entitled to a rationalization. "Everything's gotten away from me. I'm an engineer, my background is technological. I don't know anything about mysticism, about all this stuff we've gotten tangled up with. None of us were trained that way. I can't handle it. Why must I handle it? We're not qualified."

"You were the ones sent out," the voices say with an overlay of smugness, "so you are the ones to pay the price. You'll have to work out this stuff yourself. Our time is quite limited. Remember us, remember us, Evans," they say and do something to my consciousness; I feel a springing jolt deep in the skull at the place where the halves of the brain are joined, and for an instant my consciousness splits: I see myself, but then again I am inside myself; I know what I am going to say, but then again I have already said it; thrashing on the bed, I am already remembering thrashing on the bed. I reach my arms toward them: if I could only touch them and come to some final understanding, but there is no way to touch them, no way to come to terms with the Venusians, that is for sure—I have had enough trouble with the institutional staff —and then they are gone, then they are out of my head, and there is silence. "You dirty sons of bitches," I say, "I can't stand this any more, do you hear me? It isn't fair." I add, "It isn't right"; I aver, "You can't do this to me"; I suggest, "I have feelings too"; I advise and so on and so forth, but there are no answers to these very good and cogent points which I have to make, so after a while, sleep again destroyed from the night, I stagger from the bed and do the only thing which a rational man can do in relation to the situation, the only thing which makes sense and is progressive: I pull out the sheets of paper and once again I do a cryptogram.

# 57

Fumbling, I part my wife and try to enter her. I am desirous of a quick entrance, a rapid orgasm, because the weeks in heavy training and particularly the compression chamber have terrified me: I do not know if I am any longer capable of sex. My groin has been dead, dead, hanging from me loosely, small splinters of pain when I evacuate the only suggestion of remaining nerve tissue, and despite the assurances of the technicians, the advisement of the psychiatrist, I do not know if I will any longer be all right. The psychiatrist has not waited for me to bring up the subject but had broached it himself. "Some of the aspects of training may make you incapable of sex for a little while," he has said, "but it's just a temporary thing and you'll pass through it. Don't be worried about it." I have been worried about it, almost frantic in fact, but now on my first night home with my wife in several weeks things seem to be working out all right; I have managed to raise an erection, have by playing with her breasts managed to force myself into the attitudes of sexual need, and now, huffing, I poise over her, hoping that it will be possible to close my eyes and get in and out fast, without complication: find the assurance that everything is as it should be. I can worry about complications or her own satisfaction later.

She has submitted to all of this, unblinking, unspeaking, lying stone-rigid in the bed while I have played with her, her flesh curiously cool against me, having the texture of a mask which perhaps covers her real attitude, and I have wondered vaguely if there were another man, some other involvement while I was in training, and this has not so much disconcerted as excited me. I will take any image I can for the sake of sexual success: if it would enable me to come quickly, the knowledge of her adultery would only invigorate me. Now I hover over her, caught somewhere between memory and desire, looking at her closed eyes, her somnolent face, her quiet, depressed breasts, almost flat in this position, and as I dig into her I remember that it has been many years—perhaps five or six—since she has shown any sexual response whatsoever. She has cooperated, she has never denied me, but it has not gone beyond that, and I wonder if I should have discussed this subject, along with so many others, with the medical staff; I decide not because they might have simply found it grounds for disqualification. A man who cannot make his wife come is certainly incapable of achieving Venus, or so the minds of the program might think.

It does not matter, it does not matter; I push thought away from me like dust and begin to work against her, up and down, in and out, my prick moistly escaping from her several times so that I must wedge it in again, frantic with the thought that I may lose my erection. She was always very wet down there, even when she was asleep. It has nothing to do with her excitation. I know that I cannot excite her and do not even want to do it any more; all that I want to do is to come.

121

Groaning and heaving I continue to work upon her, some part of me disjointed and at odd purposes listening to all of this with detachment. There is nothing more implicitly ridiculous and humiliating than sex, which may be the reason why the program is so inconsiderate of it, but on the other hand, it is not easy to make quick judgments about the program and even though I thought I have dedicated many years to it I am still not in a position to make final decisions. As I think of this, as other things occur to me, sex seems to recede: I move out of its orbit entirely and I realize that I have been mechanically working for some moments with no progress whatsoever. For the first time she opens her eyes and looks at me. "Come, you bastard," she says, "come, for Christ's sake," and her eyes close again; I understand her loathing, see in that instant how she must be feeling about me, the exact scope of her emotions, and for some reason her contempt makes me flower. I feel myself become hard again, and sinking into necessity, falling darkly into the substance of desire, I begin to curse her, "You bitch," I say, "you lousy bitch," the closed eyes, the dead cheeks, the flat breasts, the open hole of the navel, the planes of stomach and belly rippled slightly by my own motion. "You miserable bitch," I say, and fully potent, discharge into her quarts and quarts of semen pouring out like blood, and I fall across her, meaning to hurt her with my weight but instead catch an elbow in the stomach, elbow in the ribs: pain, sudden and flaring, and groaning, I move off her. She lies there unmoving; my come pouring out of her, her limbs relaxed. She sighs, turns her head from side to side, exhales again, moves an arm to turn off the light. "You never think of anyone else," she says. "You'll always be the same, just interested in your own greedy satisfactions; you're like all the rest of them you work with, not a man but a machine," and turns from me, says no more, prepares herself for sleep.

The machine who is not a man lies there for some time thinking about what she has said, considering its connections, bolts, housing, informational centers. It inputs data and it outputs further questions; more data goes in and questions come forth, still more data but no answers; there are no answers. The machine sighs. It thinks of the compression chamber. It thinks of the Captain. It thinks of Venus. It thinks of its own abused genitals, dangling beneath it now like wiring torn from the bulkhead. Eventually it thinks no more. It closes down. It reduces its circuit load. It cancels input. It sleeps.

# 58

*A Short History of the Space Program:* The space program was invented in 1960 for political purposes and flourished through that decade, culminating in the landing upon the moon in 1969. Subsequent moon expeditions followed, but the political climate, initially favorable to the program, had turned and a severe cutback in appropriations, aided by public hostility, resulted in the 1973 shutdown of the moon program with only the continuance of two manned capsules; in 1976, with a vastly decreased budget and minimal publicity, the Mars expedition was hastily formulated and sent on its way in the belief that the successful landing on Mars would save both the program and the administration from the consequences of internal disorders; Mars did not work out so well, however, so in 1981 the first manned flight to Venus was made instead: two men in a small, somewhat underpowered capsule believed capable of direct landing upon Venus and subsidiary use as an experimental base of operations; the Venus flight, however, also ran into certain difficulties.

In 1981, at the age of twenty-one, the space program ended, having attained the necessary majority and then expiring.

# 59

*A Short History of Harry M. Evans:* Harry M. Evans was born in 1943 to rigorous Protestant stock in upstate New York; he attended local schools and the Pittsburgh College of Engineering, where he obtained an advanced degree in metallurgy and electronics before entering the Air Force in 1968 as a second lieutenant. Rising to the rank of major by 1972, due to his superb facility in test flights and his excellent sense of timing, Harry M. Evans applied to the program for admission and was accepted in 1974. He worked in backup crews, checkout flights and general processes at the program and was a member of the fifth alternate crew for the Mars expedition. Applying for the Venus project in 1980, by all objective criteria Harry M. Evans was found to be the second most qualified man in the program and was the copilot on the first Venus run in collaboration with his Captain, Jack Josephson, who in 1981 fell into the sun.

In 1967 Harry M. Evans was married to Helen K. Williams in Pittsburgh, Pennsylvania. She led me on quite a great deal but would not let me actually fuck her until we were engaged. It was only at that time that I suspected that we would not have an entirely successful sexual relationship, but it was too late by then. Harry M. Evans, who came from rigorous Protestant stock, did not believe in indiscriminate or promiscuous fornication, and thus she was able to handle me in that way.

Helen K. Williams was the motivating force in the life of Harry M. Evans. She was responsible for his enlistment in the Air Force and for his subsequent application to the program. I had to do something to get away from her. As a sacrificing and understanding wife she stood by his side all through the series of events which culminated in the honor of his selection to the Venus ship. Things reached such a point that Venus seemed more accessible than her.

Harry M. Evans successfully completed his mission to Venus; that is to say, he got out in that vicinity and then he came back. Today, at the age of thirty-eight, Evans lives at the above address where on indefinite leave from the program he is working on his memoirs which under a pen name are scheduled to be published by Random House in the spring of 1982.

# 60

"Events," I say to the Captain, "events control our lives, although we have no understanding of them nor do they have any motivation. Everything is blind chance, happenstance, occurrence; in an infinite universe anything can happen. After the fact we find reasons. We're going to Venus because the dice came up."

"Yes," he says. He says this quietly, no ceremony or celebration in his tone; a curious air of anticlimax for all the excitement of this moment. "Yes, you're right. That's it. You finally hit it. That is the true and real reason we're going to Venus. Definitely. Very good." He stands, brushes small pieces of imagined lint from his rumpled clothing. "That completes the first round of the game," he says. "I believe I'll shit."

"That's all? It's my turn now."

"Yes, of course it's your turn now, but we're going to take a break. We've been at this for hours."

"I don't care *how* long we've been at it. It's my turn now and I want to go."

"Oh, for God's sake," the Captain says, shaking his head, "you have no realism, no consideration. I said I have to shit. Then we'll have a rest and after that will be time enough to play the game if you want."

"If I want!" I say. I rise. It is the first time I have been in a standing position for many hours and my joints are stiff, small flares of pain and discovery lighting up the connections as I advance toward him. "You son of a bitch," I say, "you're not being fair. You said that I was to go first and then you would go. We're going to go now. I have a question to ask you."

"Not now."

"You led me on and led me on and finally when I win, you don't want to play. I don't have to take that," I shriek, "even if you are the Captain! Besides, I never liked you anyway, if you want to know the truth. You're a stolid, stupid son of a bitch and you have no sensitivity at all."

"Control yourself, Evans."

"You're the best living example of what the program develops: there's nothing inside you except to take punishment—that capacity, nothing else—and now you won't even play by the rules of your own stupid game!" I am quite distraught. "I should kill you for this," I point out. "You deserve to die."

"This is mutiny, Evans."

"Mutiny?" I say. Shouting, I stumble after the Captain as he moves slowly to one of the cubicles in which we deposit our sanitized waste; the waste to be retained until we move into the orbit of Venus, when the greater gravity will attract it and we can fling our feces toward that planet. "Are you serious? Do you believe this? I have questions to ask you!" and raving, I pick up a wrench from the bulkhead. "I'll show you evacuation," I say, quite possessed now, quite beyond reason, "I'll show you what you can do with your goddamned rules and games and orders," and I hoist the wrench, pivot, move toward him, hit him a shattering blow in the temple.

His head explodes; small filaments briefly become a halo in

the harsh lighting. Everything that they said about the temple was true; it is apparently a very sensitive spot. The Captain is dead before he can even come to terms with it; he barks one syllable— something that sounds like *wowl*—and then falls before me, landing heavily on his belly, instinctively pulling up his knees: he looks like a man ready for fucking. This strikes my sense of humor; I giggle, and as I giggle, I drag him to the disposal chute, the load enormously lightened by my merriment, my amusement, my relief at finally having solved the Captain Problem. "It's fair, it's fair, it was the only thing to do," I sing as I open the hatchway, stump the corpse into the chute, pull up the handle, and with a press of a lever send him on his way. "You wouldn't play by your own rules; there's nothing to be done with you then, and besides that," I say, stricken with an idea, "besides, this will solve the whole Venusian problem; now we're done with you and I can get the ship back. I'll say the Venusians killed you; I wouldn't want the disgrace of you having been killed by an assistant," I confide to the chute and turn, with only a slight hitch in my walk now as limbs revise, move to the console, and begin to work out a program for returning. I think of sending a message back explaining the circumstances but decide not to. It would only disconcert them and they would not understand (as I am only beginning to understand at this instant) that the Captain wanted to die, that his death was predetermined not only by the Venusians but by the program, and that in giving him exactly what he wanted, I had helped him toward ascension. There is no way they will see that for a long long time, I think—humming as I play with the relays—but I will help them: when I return, I will explain it to them over and over again and eventually they will see and they will be very happy and as always everything will work out for the best as inevitably it must in a world which can view Venus, will it, and then make confrontation.

# 61

"That's all?" Forrest says to Evans. "You mean, that's all
there is?" and with a growl, Evans leaps upon the fat man, bears
him to the ground, begins to choke the life out of him, the web-
bing of the neck pasty and shriveled; Forrest an even older man
than he thought. "What do you want?" Evans murmurs as he
strangles Forrest to death. "What do you want, easy answers?
You send me to Venus, you put me through all of this, and you
want anything final?" and Forrest begins to whimper for pity,
beg for release, explain (although he is strangling, somehow able
to talk) that he was only following orders and that in the personal
way he wishes Evans the best and would like him to stop forth-
with, but Evans, quite mad, is beyond any interventions of reason
or Forrest or anyone else: they are alone in the room, Evans
chokes him, Forrest dies; Evans breaks his neck, Forrest dies;
Evans shatters his medulla with a backhanded chop and Forrest
dies; Evans mounts him like a horse and rides him to suffocation
and Forrest dies; again and again he dies again and again Evans
kills him—curiously satisfying it is, being able to work one's will
at last. Forrest dies, Forrest dies: the attendants stand by the wall
rubbing their hands and muttering to one another. They look
pleased. They do not seem to have any objections. They are protected by the Civil Service Ever Horizons program and in the
bargain, Evans senses, it is possible that Forrest has been giving
them as difficult a time as him. *Wow!,* Forrest groans under Evans
and becomes the Captain, the Captain dies too; both Forrest and
the Captain die together, two for the price of one, and oh, oh, oh,
the satisfaction of it!

# 62

Coming into the green planet, hitting the orbit for the first time, I found myself staring at the porthole, the one away from the sun (because the sun would kill us and thus the porthole in that direction was always automatically shielded—wondrous technology), and seeing the impenetrable gas even this deep in, found myself saying: *Impossible, this is too much, this cannot be* and similar reassurances as the craft settled into a five-hundred-mile declension and then began slowly to bail out, reaching a five-hundred-mile apogee and then so on; standing there, the mission accomplished, the planet at last green and clotted before us, I found myself no more capable than I had been at the beginning, the very beginning, to deal with it. *Impossible,* I said, and *impossible* again while the machinery of the craft burbled about its manic tasks and I heard small crackling inquiries from the monitor. They wanted to know how we were doing. They wanted to know if we had settled after the transmission blackout. I shut it off. It was the only way.

And stood there then still looking at Venus; Venus imponderable, not knowing the quality of my desire or even, under the circumstances, if I could judge it, and at that moment I found myself quite naturally addressing my old friend X, who through coincidence or not was standing beside me watching the slow, tumbling glaze of the planet, none the worse for the wear although bearing some slight psychic damage from his experiences; damage which I could grasp from the core and this was peculiar because I had never been credited nor had I credited myself with that much perception.

"Impossible," I repeated to him, "that's what I've been

thinking," and socially offered him a tranquilizer, another from the diminished store I had been sitting over since the Venusian Disaster, and X took one absently, placed it in his mouth and chewing said, "But this is nothing new. I've seen it all before. It's the same."

"It can't be," I said, struck by the sadness in his eyes, a maturity and penitence which I had never expected in the youthful and rather impetuous X, "everything is different. You went to Mars, but this is Venus and I don't know what to do. Do you understand that? I have no idea."

"Mars," X said, "Venus, it's all the same; the quality of the experience is all the same. I hear that they felt the same way on the moon. No, it's too late, Evans, too late to make simple judgments or even to measure your life against them; you must assume a larger perspective and put it from you like all the other childish things." He grasped my elbow, strength flooding from him into me. "These are all abstractions," he said. "You won't understand that for a long time, but that is all they are. It's not what you see; it's the distance you have to travel, and you'll understand that just as I have." And pressed my elbow, winked at me with a conspiratorial air, and was gone.

"Come back," I said, "you can't leave me alone like this; I've got things to do, a decision to make, come back, damn it," but he was gone, indisputably gone, just as the others—the Captain, my wife—had gone and nothing to do but to curse the loss and get on to other things. "Fuck you, you son of a bitch," I said and other similarly unreasonable things, "you lousy bastard," and so on and so forth, but eventually, as the ship wound around in its orbit, became purposeful again and decided that at all costs, I had to run out the mission for its own sake. "I wanted to change lives," I found myself saying again, just like the first time. "I wanted to change the way in which we saw ourselves. I wanted to irretrievably alter the contents of our reactions. It must not end this way, it can not end this way," but as we swung around into the third orbit, it occurred to me that it was highly likely that it would; that this above all would be the most logical and interlocking outcome of all which had preceded, and that there was nothing to say to that, nothing at all. "Come back, X!" I pleaded. "Show me what to do now," but in the craft nothing, in the air nothing, and I understood then and finally that on Venus or the earth, in the void or in the mud, one had to make one's own decisions and live by them, and the simple banality of this aphorism—I wish to assure you gentlemen—drove me quite mad, although not as mad as the Captain, who while throwing out some wastes had a slight accident with the disposal hatch and fell into the sun.

## 63

HARRY M EVANS
H MARRY VENAS
H MARRY VENAS
VENAS MARRY H

## 64

"I'm frightened," the Captain said. "Can't you understand that? I can't be your crutch any more. I'm terrified; I can't take this. Please, Evans, leave me alone."

"No," I said, lunging from my seat to seize his trembling form and hold it against me, curiously aging and pathetic in the hot spaces of the capsule, "you can't be frightened. I need you! I've depended on you! All my life I've depended upon institutions, authority to carry me through. You can't do this to me now; you're the only institution I have. Think of our responsibilities. Think of the flight."

"I can't take it any more," he said, "I'm terrified. I'm sick of your dependency, I'm sick of myself. Of everything. I never wanted to go to Venus. I never wanted any part of it; they forced me into it. I was preselected, the tests were a farce. I never took the tests. *You* passed them, Evans: you're more qualified than I am. So you find the solution. You resolve this."

"No," I said, holding on to him more tightly, running my hands over the back of his neck, "it can't be that way. You're the Captain. I've got to follow your orders."

"I'm sorry," he said, detaching himself from me, his hands clawlike as he ripped free of my embrace, "I'm sorry, but I can't cut this any more; it's not your fault, it's mine, Evans; you'll have to deal with this the best way you can." And before I could stop him, astonishment mingling with terror in me to hold me fast, he stumbled to the evacuation capsule and placed himself within. "I've gone mad," he said to me. "That will be the explanation I want you to give. Tell them that I went mad. Don't tell them that I couldn't take it any more and that I'm perfectly sane, because they will never be able to accept that and they will torture you terribly. No more, Evans, no more," he said and closed the lid. I heard the whisper of machinery; in an instant he was gone.

In an instant the Captain was gone, I was alone, there was nothing for me to do. Alone, always alone; I knew that it would be in this way. At the end of all the machinery, the training, the instructions, and the pain would come this moment at the end of the tube when, still and vacant, I would confront the dead panels of the console and understand that somehow, anyhow, I had to work it out for myself.

# 65

*Commercial Mysticism:* Commercial mysticism was invented in the mid-1960's as a reaction against the devices of technology and particularly of the space program, which gave more and more people the feeling that their lives were totally out of control and that there was no way in which they could stop machines from crushing them to death. The occult, the bizarre, satanism, astrology, and the factors of chance reached high popularity during this difficult period, which still continues. Demonology became extant, as did the tarot and the Book of Changes, the *I Ching*.

One of the theories of the new mystics was that all of space was merely a projection of the inner wastes of man and that space exploration therefore became merely another and dull metaphor for internal exploration: up against Mars, Venus, Ceres or the moon the voyager was merely confronting one or another pyramid reared in his own damaged psyche. Under this theory, the rationalization for space exploration became preposterous. One would have been better off accepting from the beginning the internal truth of oneself or, failing that, seeking competent care in an institution where for relaxation cryptograms, hairgrayers, puzzles, and sexual biography would serve the essential purposes while keeping allotted time free for introspection and the consideration of inner space.

# 66

Evans and I meet. We have been looking for one another for a long time; now the moment has come and we join hands in the darkness. "Pleased ta meetcha," says Evans and I say the same; we mumble courtesies to one another, knowing that there is no need to discuss larger issues. We understand everything. We have lived together, although behind barriers, for so long.

"We must tell them," Evans says, and I agree. "We must tell them," I say and without a further word we walk to the door and open it. It is no longer barred; we can walk through these halls at will. "Tell them how it was," Evans says and I add, "and how it will always be," and we chuckle at one another companionably. There are no misunderstandings. There could not possibly be, considering our relationship, the roots we have established.

We walk down the hall hand in hand, strollers out for a nightcap, whistling at the beams. "I think that this is right," Evans says. "We can't hold it back forever. Sooner or later they would have to know."

"Yes," I say, "they would have to know sooner or later, and anyway, it's not our fault. We aren't responsible. It's just a question of telling them what happened."

"Exactly," says Evans. He runs a finger against my palm tentatively, as close to an embrace as two well-adjusted men can come. "By the way," he says, "how was your sex life? Was it okay? Did you get yours?"

"No," I say. "It was lousy."

"That's interesting. So was mine."

"I think it had something to do with the program. They made a machine of me."

"That's interesting again. I happened to be in the program as well and was thinking exactly the same thing. It's nice to know that we're on the same track."

"Yes," I say, "yes," and Evans and I stroll toward the end of the corridor, knock authoritatively on the door for an attendant. There will be an attendant. There has always been an attendant. After a time the door is opened and, blinking, we emerge into the light, nodding cordially at the keeper of the door. I notice that there are small beads of moisture on Evans' face. Probably there are some on mine as well. It is damp and uncomfortable in these rooms despite the fumbling attempts they make at climate control. "We have something to say," I say to the attendant. "Both of us, that is."

"Yes," says Evans, "and we'd like to say it quickly. Time is money, you know, and you want to get that second expedition off as quickly as possible, don't you?"

"Wait," the attendant says, "wait," and scurries off, making placating gestures behind him. We stand, quite calmly and at ease, looking at the iron, the gates, the walkways, the loudspeakers.

"Strange," I say, "you seem to have been on the Venus expedition."

"Indeed I was."

"So was I."

"How about that?" Evans says. "How about that? Isn't that interesting?" and we nod at each other cordially again, and in due time the attendant returns. Behind him is the man whom I know as Claude Forrest. He has been aroused from sleep and his face is pale with disorientation. He looks at us standing in the hall. "All right," he says. "Yes. Yes? Tell me. Is this something new or is this the same thing yet again?"

"New," I say, motioning Evans to be silent, showing him that I, who know Forrest well, will handle the situation. "Entirely new. The end of it."

"Well, then," he says, "out with it." He takes a handkerchief from his pocket, wipes his face up and down, across and through, like a viewplate. "Tell me. I want to know. I'm waiting. What do you have to say?"

"I want to tell you the full and final truth of the voyage. The treatment is complete now; I remember everything. And I will tell you."

"Tell me," he says, "tell me then," and leans toward me with a feral expression. "Let me know; let me know."

"Yes," I say, winking at Evans, my collaborator in the eternal and finally achieved search for truth, "I will." And begin then to tell him.

# 67

"I loved the Captain in my own way, although I knew that he was insane, the poor bastard," I say. "This was only partly his fault: one must consider the conditions. The conditions were intolerable."

And realize then what I have said. Forrest sighs, Evans sighs, the attendant sighs, they crumple in the hall, and I can see from the dull glare in Forrest's eyes that it is hopeless, quite hopeless. He will never understand. None of them will understand. And I do not know the language to teach them.

"This will never work," I say.

# Epilogue

Mr. Harry M. Evans
c/o Sunderland
1836 Longacre Street
Middle Village, Illinois

Dear Mr. Evans:

I am pleased to inform you that all of us here are delighted with your manuscript, *Beyond Apollo*, and we would like to make a formal offer of publication. Our standard contract is being drawn up and will be in your hands by the end of the month.

Several questions of format will have to be resolved, of course. Although you state in your covering letter that you are "feeling much better now and doubt the objective truth of much of this diary" so that perhaps you "ought to publish it as a novel" if we want to publish it, we all feel here that *Beyond Apollo* should be a work of nonfiction. You have a fascinating story to tell of the ill-fated Venus expedition, one which can only add to the scanty knowledge already available, and we think that as the first-person account of the only living human being who ever *went* to Venus it could be enormously popular.

I am sure that minor copyediting and editorial adjustments can eliminate many of those "apparent inconsistencies" to which you refer and will produce a tight, pleasing, first-person account of the way your "mission" looked to *you* at a time of some emotional maladjustment. We are, of course, ideally equipped to publish *Beyond Apollo* successfully and think that we can look forward to extensive foreign sales, a selection by a good book club, and perhaps even a movie or cassette option. Our excellent subsidiary rights department will follow up all of these possibilities, of course, and since our contract will enable us to share such subsidiaries equally, you can be sure that we will be doing our best!

For the moment I wish to thank you very much for sending your manuscript our way, and I offer my best regards to you and that patient and dedicated lady whom you refer to in your covering letter as "the light of my life, my wife."

Very truly yours,

*K. Martin Conrad*
Senior Editor

KMC/lh
cc: Dr. Claude Forrest